TWO SISTERS
WRITING & PUBLISHING™

First Annual
Anthology

featuring
International Writers

TWO SISTERS

WRITING & PUBLISHING™

First Annual
Anthology

featuring
International Writers

Catherine M. Greenspan
& Elizabeth Ann Atkins

Editors

For information about this title or to order other books
and/or electronic media, contact the publisher:

Two Sisters Writing and Publishing™
2340 Hwy 180 East, Suite 244
Silver City, NM 88061

ISBN 978-1-945875-21-2 (Paperback)
ISBN 978-1-945875-22-9 (eBook)

First Edition

Cover and Interior design: Van-garde Imagery, Inc.
Editorial Assistant: Reema Baydoun

Printed in the United States of America

Dedication

This anthology is dedicated to all aspiring writers in general and to the writers who believed in themselves and their work – and clicked the SUBMIT button.

"Easy reading is damn hard writing."

~ Nathaniel Hawthorne

Contents

"El Duende"

by Casandra Hernández Ríos

The day a duende appeared in Emilio's room, he ran to tell his mother and father, but they looked at him with disappointment and shook their heads. They told him it was just his imagination, but Emilio insisted. He tugged at his father's sleeve until he gave in and agreed to look under the bed, where Emilio had seen the small, child-like creature. His father lifted the twin mattress from its frame and slid the wooden slots out of the way for a better look, but no duende. His father repositioned the slots, fit the mattress back, and sat on the edge of Emilio's bed.

It hadn't always been this way, but for the past year, Emilio's father spent a lot of time explaining that gnomes, monsters, or creatures from his grandfather's stories couldn't be dreamed into reality. "Your abuelito told me the same bedtime tales when I was your age, but they're just that—tales and stories," his father said. Emilio caught himself beginning to re-explain, but he could see his father's patience had thinned by the way he looked and spoke at him. Both of his parents looked at him differently, but he couldn't remember when it first happened. He just knew they had two ways of looking, the one they had for him and the one they had for Carmen, his baby sister.

Weeks passed and with each sighting, Emilio came to know the duende. He had a mischievous laugh, the kind of laugh Emilio had heard at school, a laugh shared by playground bullies. But Emilio didn't feel intimidated by the creature, he felt at ease, actually, when in his company. The mysterious creature had become his guest and Emilio tried to feed him, but the duende never ate the pan Dulce or milk that Emilio left for him. Emilio only caught glimpses of the duende, but was able to put together mental images to form a complete picture. The duende ran on skinny legs, the pant hems were closer to his knees than his ankles, and his large belly prominently featured its belly button. If Emilio had been more brave, he would have tried to capture him to clothe him, but like him, the duende was doing just fine on his own.

Most afternoons, he spent them in his room flipping through story books his grandfather had left behind for a clue as to why the duende had chosen Emilio, or he'd imagine being able to have a conversation with the duende and be able to ask him himself. Other times, when his mother didn't push him to leave his room for dinner, Emilio would sleep through afternoons. There were some days when he was overcome by an unexplained exhaustion and he'd tell his mother he couldn't eat or go to school because he was tired. It wasn't a lie; he was tired. He thought the weight of keeping quiet about the duende had exhausted him. But he didn't want to get rid of the duende, for when Emilio wasn't home, all he could do was look for the duende in quiet corners, in the depths of shadows. He yearned for his company and the warmth he felt by being near the creature.

Winter and summer break always brought his grandfather back to Emilio. His grandpa lived in Guadalajara, six hours northwest from where Emilio's family lived in México City. Because his grandfather lives so far away, he'd stay a week or two at a time with the family. He had always looked forward to his grandfather's visit, even if it meant having to go to church on Sundays and having to sit on rigid pew benches. The awkwardness he felt, as he sat among people wearing their best clothes and best behavior, while they prayed or spoke softly to an invisible entity Emilio knew nothing about, would cause him to feel small. When his grandfather asked Emilio how he wanted to spend his domingo, the ten pesos his grandfather gave him after church to spend that day, he'd say "Xochimilco!"

Lake Xochimilco was Emilio's favorite place in the world. He had grown up hearing stories about the people his grandfather had met when he worked there on a chinampa, growing flowers and selling them to tourists, and about how during that time of his grandfather, he spent more time floating on water than on land.

Before the duende, getting up on Sundays wasn't difficult. His grandfather would always knock on Emilio's room and Emilio would open the door, wearing a long sleeve shirt and pants his mother had picked out for him the night before. But this morning, Emilio's mother had to drag Emilio from bed and help him into his clothes because his grandfather was waiting for him.

"I'm really tired," Emilio said, dragging his feet as they made their way from his room toward the front door. "Please let me stay home."

"What's wrong with you?" she said. "You love going with your grandfather. It'll do you some good to leave the house for once." She crossed her arms.

He plumped on the front steps, surrendering to his fate. He felt his shirt's collar tighten and his sweater suffocate him. He unfastened the top buttons and pulled his clothes away from his neck.

"Oh, it's okay," his grandfather said, as he emerged from the house. "Let him stay. I can come back after church and take him to Xochimilco." He smiled at Emilio and began to cross the yard toward the main highway.

His mother shook her head in disappointment. Emilio remained on the front steps, as he watched his grandfather disappear around a building.

His grandfather returned after church for Emilio, as he promised, and collected him and Carmen for the trip to Xochimilco. Emilio wanted to oppose Carmen's company, but he knew that it wasn't up for discussion. Now that the three were on the main pathway into Xochimilco, that morning's events felt silly. Emilio watched his grandfather and Carmen walk hand-in-hand several feet ahead of him. He felt better and was relieved to know that his grandfather wasn't mad at him. He had also managed to get the duende off his mind. But he couldn't leave him behind—not completely—because every now and then, Emilio thought he heard the duende's laugh. Every time he heard the sound, he turned and looked around, but no duende in sight. He only saw other children running circles around their parents.

"Look at the pretty flowers!" Carmen said, bouncing in place.

She turned to look back at Emilio. Her face was glowing. He hadn't noticed how pretty she looked in yellow, the color of the dress she was wearing, but he wouldn't tell her. She was three, but her features had sharpened, and Emilio could already imagine what she would look like when she turned his age. She had captured their parent's gaze and soon his grandfather's.

"Emi, Emi, look at the pretty flowers!" His sister was pointing at a woman in a chalupa, selling flowers.

"Yeah, yeah, I see them," he said and rolled his eyes. He wasn't in the mood to put up with her. She had already ruined the day by tagging along. Couldn't she just leave him alone?

They continued walking until the the road forked, one side leading to a dock where trajineras, draped in red, yellow or blue paint, were anchored. The other path led them back home. Normally, they took a ride on the canal. But today was different. His grandfather stopped and thought for a moment. He looked at Emilio.

"Let's get some raspados and rest for a bit," he said. Emilio nodded. Carmen pointed at a man grating a large block of ice and pulled their grandfather toward him. They ordered a lemon-flavored raspado for each and then walked over to a bench facing the edge of the lake. Emilio found the sun's reflection on the lake's wavering surface and wondered if the light was strong enough to blind someone.

"Abuelito? Do you believe in duendes?" Emilio said, afraid that his grandfather would snap at him for asking. Emilio raised his brows expectantly. His grandfather was eating the raspado with a plastic spoon.

"Sure," he said, and took another spoonful of lemon-flavored ice.

Emilio looked down at his cup filled to the brim, the grated ice melting into the green-colored juice.

"Carmen, sweetie, why don't you go see if there are fish in the lake. You don't have to get too close to the water," his grandfather said, pointing with his chin toward the edge of the water.

Carmen smiled and began walking toward the lake, taking small, steady steps.

"There. That's close enough, sweetie" his grandfather said. She stopped and bent her knees to lean in for a closer look. Emilio watched her. For a moment, he imagined her falling, face-first, into the water. The thought startled him.

"I'm going to tell you a story, but it has to stay between us. Do you understand? Your mother mentioned your duende and she was pretty upset," his grandfather said.

"Okay, I won't tell her, or anyone else, I promise," Emilio said. It seemed like his grandfather believed him, and Emilio felt relieved.

"When I was about your age, ten or so, I saw two small children playing in the fields from the tree I had climbed that morning. They wove their dancing between the maguey plants, their one-piece gowns were the same color, as the dry soil below their bare feet. I wouldn't have noticed them if I hadn't heard their laughter. It was light and musical, like watercolors. I could have watched them all day from behind the curtain of leaves and branches."

"And did you?" Emilio said, leaning in.

"I took my gaze from them for a second when I heard my mother calling. And then they were gone. When I told my mother what I had seen, she said they were duendes, and warned me to stay away," his grandfather said. "Have you seen any fish, sweetie?"

"Not yet, abuelito," Carmen said.

"Why did she say that?" Emilio asked anxiously.

"Because she met them when she was a child. They tried to take her, but she knew their tricks."

"What tricks?"

"Well, they convince children to play their games, and sometimes these games last for days. They invited my mother into the forest to see their house, but she said no and ran as fast as she could, leaving the sound of their laughter behind. They're naughty little things," his grandfather said. "Come on, Carmen, it's time to go."

"I don't believe it," Emilio said, crossing his arms. It was the first time he didn't want to believe one of his grandfather's story. He couldn't imagine duendes as evil. Maybe the duende hid Emilio's shoes or spilled all of his Legos on the carpet, but the duende would never harm anyone. Besides, the duende never left his room, and was too shy to even show himself. He'd never trick anyone.

His grandfather shrugged and led Carmen around the bench by the hand. Emilio stood from his seat and followed them. He was feeling better, his feet were light, and he wasn't as tired as before. He didn't like his grandfather's story, but at least he believed that duendes were real.

They took the path home and walked for some time along the rim of the lake, until the path began to narrow and ascend. Their grandfather let go of Carmen to walk in front because the three of them didn't fit. Emilio was still holding Carmen's hand. She kept looking over the edge, down at the deep irrigation channels that veined from the lake.

He knew it was a bad idea when he let go of his sister's hand to tie his loose shoestring, as soon as he did it. Carmen began pointing at something over the edge that Emilio couldn't see from where he was. He heard her say, "Flower. Look at that flower," softly, as if whispering to herself, and continued to lean closer and closer over the edge.

Emilio started to tell Carmen to wait for him, when she fell forward without a sound. She didn't scream, nor cry. She was only a few feet from him. It all happened fast. He shuffled toward her and found her, hanging from the side of of the channel, the murky water below, with nothing to hold on to. He lay on his stomach, to be as low as possible to the ground, and reached for his sister's hand, but she was out of reach.

That was when he saw it: the flower his sister had been pointing at. It was a bright color blue, a strange, but wonderful contrast to the dark greens and browns of Xochimilco's wetlands. The flower was beautiful and captivating. He heard music in his ear sing,

"Hold on to the flower." Emilio repeated the words:

"Hold on to the flower." He waited for Carmen to begin to reach for the flower's stem. "I'll go get help, just hold on," he said.

Emilio wasn't sure why he waited for a nod or for her to say something. Tears raced down her cheeks, but she didn't make a sound. She looked frightened. Emilio couldn't see the girl who had captured their parent's gaze and now his grandfather's anymore. When he saw her take hold of the flower's stem, Emilio rose to his feet. He saw his grandfather in the distance. It was strange how far he was from them. He would have to yell or run after him to get his attention. He began to take a deep breath to call for his grandfather when he heard the duende's laugh. It was different; it was tinged with something Emilio couldn't recognize, but he knew it wasn't good.

Emilo's heart fell into his stomach. He looked back at his sister, hanging from the channel's slick sides from a single stem, and realized what he had done. Through foggy eyes, he watched as the stem snapped, dropping his sister into the water. The splash didn't sound, and if it did, he didn't hear it. He stood there, watching the water calm from where it had been disturbed, cradling the blue-petalled flower.

©2016 Casandra Hernández Ríos

About the Author: Casandra Hernández Ríos received her MFA in Creative Writing, Fiction, from CSU Long Beach. She holds a BA in Creative Writing and Journalism from the same school. She is former Senior Managing Editor at The Offing magazine, and former Editor-in-Chief of Riprap, CSU Long Beach's literary journal. In 2015, she was recognized as an emerging writer at Long Beach's Literary Women Festival of Authors. Her work has appeared in The Acentos Review, the Santa Ana River Review, Verdad magazine, and American Mustard. She teaches at Golden West College and Long Beach City College.

"The Blind Oasis"

by Anthony Johnson

The itch behind June's ear burrowed into the pulpy sponge of her brain like a clicking beetle. The irritating sensation began the evening she had dropped a wreath of azaleas into the ocean from the very same barnacled dock her brother had jumped from exactly a year before.

Her mother, ever fussy, had suggested June drop lilies instead. Azaleas are more of a love flower, the heavyset woman had told her. They're usually meant for women.

In the end, June stuck with azaleas, and after watching the pink wreath spin atop a green whirlpool before vanishing into its depths, she dropped herself into the seething sea.

Pushing off from the pillars of the pier, June swam desperately for shore, fighting against the invisible pull of the waves until her eyes bulged and her muscles burned from exhaustion. Once ashore, she stretched out on the beachhead and napped in the angry stare of the sun.

The next morning, June discovered the itch quietly gnawing beneath her right ear, her favorite of the two. Thinking it nothing more than an errant bit of sand and seawater, she did her best to dislodge it with her finger. But this only seemed to increase the muffled buzz and, accordingly, increase her irritation.

At breakfast, she complained to her mother of her predicament in hope that she might offer some sort of sage remedy only a mother would have knowledge of. The itch was a constant presence in the background of her thoughts and tinted her mood a deep shade of blue. June was sure she'd go mad if she didn't find a solution soon.

Have you tried shaking your head repeatedly, her mother suggested. Like when you really don't want to eat something?

June gave it a shot, shaking her head until she became dizzy and nearly fell over onto the floor. The remedy seemed to work at first, but the moment the room regained its equilibrium, the itch rebounded and continued on with its bothersome clawing.

Her mother then tried attacking the itch with a Q-tip. She dug with the confident thoroughness of a miner, and not two minutes later she stopped and said aloud,

Now what do we have here?

June tried to glance around the side of her head as her mother inserted a pair of tweezers into her ear and removed a long gleaming string out of the girl's head.

Tell me what it is, June said impatiently. Tell me what it is.

It's just some sort of string.

Gross! Pull it out! Pull it out!

June's mother did as she was told. But the more she pulled, the more string inexplicably came forth. Pretty soon, a spool of several feet lay wound in her mother's hand. She then tried cutting it with a pair of scissors and when that too failed, she tried burning it off with a lit match. Nothing she did, however, had any effect whatsoever.

What am I supposed to do? June whined. I can't go to school with a string hanging out of my head.

I have a plan, but you probably won't like it, her mother said. The older woman wrapped the string several times about her daughter's head and tucked it beneath the girl's black hair. There you go, she said, satisfied. Good as new.

June's mother had made an appointment with the girl's doctor the following week to address the spider web-thin string coming out of her daughter's ear. But after two days spent in the torture of her classmates, her mother managed to get the appointment pushed up to the following Thursday.

Once they had discovered the string, June's classmates had been unable to resist pulling on it at every opportunity. They grabbed it during class, yanked on it while standing in line for lunch, and the sophomores even made a game of grabbing the string and running up and down the hallways with it. It took June so long to bundle up the string that she was late for class and received detention from the vice principal.

The girls, however, were the worst. A gang of the more popular ones caught June alone in the bathroom, forced her into a stall, and tied her to a toilet with a series of knots so tangled and intricate the janitor had to be paged to set the poor, sobbing girl free.

June's doctor was a pipsqueak of a man who wore telescope glasses and a silver mustache so bushy it looked as if a ferret had curled up under his nose and fallen asleep. Indeed, the man was so short, he had to stand atop a stool in order to peer into June's ear with his otoscope.

Hmm…yes…I see, he mumbled. He set the otoscope down and proceeded to pull out great lengths of the sparkling string from

June's ear. Minutes later, a pile of the spooled string rose up from the floor right up to the doctor's ankles.

See that you don't fish out her brain, Doctor, June's mother said cheekily.

Of course not, replied the doctor. Nothing to worry about. Nothing at all. He let go of the string and pretended to consult June's chart.

We'll just need to run a few tests. He then backed out of the room in a rather obvious attempt of escape. Moments later, a nurse came into the room with a hospital gown and the announcement that June would be staying the night, so her condition could be, quote-unquote, monitored more closely.

June spent the following month in the hospital and was systematically moved from room to room, wing to wing, so she could be examined by every doctor, specialist, expert, and practically anyone else in the hospital who had a qualified opinion. One by one, she was paraded before audiologists, neurologists, oncologists, and once, even, a surly dentist who knew nothing of the string growing out of June's ear. Quite frankly, he couldn't give two damns, as he, himself, put it. But he recommended, anyway, that she have her wisdom teeth removed soon, or she ran the risk of them becoming impacted.

And so it went, for weeks on end. With each visit by a new doctor, the string was unraveled more and more. Some doctors only removed a few feet, while others would pull out long reams, stretching yards and yards of it out in an inexhaustible supply, each hell-bent on being the doctor who reached the end of the seemingly infinite fiber.

One night, weeks into her stay, June muted the documentary she was watching about the Great Valley Mountains in the northern country and asked her mother if she was going to die.

Her mother put down the sweater she was crocheting out of the excess string and told her plainly,

Of course not, dear. I'd like to think I'm not unlucky enough a mother to lose both of my children. Now get some sleep, we have another dozen appointments tomorrow.

On and on, the doctors came in a parade of starched lab coats, each picking, poking, and prodding her with questions, fingers, and needles until she felt like a human porcupine.

Flanked by a battalion of doctors, she made the cover of Medical Maladies Monthly, and a million-dollar prize was even offered by Milton Moses Morrison, the notorious billionaire and space travel magnate who was known widely in the medical community for his interest in outlandish illnesses. The more bizarre the condition, the more he invested in its scrutiny.

In the end, no solution was found, and the string continued to be unspooled all throughout the winter and deep into the following spring. June had lost considerable weight during this period and lay in her hospital bed like a pale and brittle seashell.

Days before the start of summer, a possible solution arrived from the most unlikely of places. June was close to giving up hope of ever leaving the hospital when a peculiar elderly woman emerged from the thick fog of doctors and began prodding her in the stomach with a stick so smooth and black, that June mistook it for a taxidermy snake. Upon closer examination, June realized the stick was, in fact, a stupefied cottonmouth, long charmed into its rigid position. She was amazed to see its beady copper eyes were still alive and flicking about the hospital room.

The woman herself was of an even stranger appearance. She wore a spotted giraffe coat, had a hairy face and a crooked nose, and her glossy opal eyes were so steady and focused, June came to trust the woman after just one look. And she continued trusting the strange woman even after glancing down and seeing the heads of two baby alligators gawping up at her from the woman's feet.

The elderly woman proceeded to examine June in the most curious manner. She peered up her nostrils, smelled her hair, and even touched a drop of the girl's spit to her tongue. When she did finally speak, the room fell into a quick silence.

I am a witch doctor from deep in the swamp, she declared in a voice so pointed, that several of the doctors shivered from an imagined cold. I have a potential cure for your illness, but it comes with great risk, more risk than you can possibly imagine. If we are to continue forward, I must have your word that my instructions will be followed to the letter and most importantly, with complete trust. What say you? Do you still have courage in this husk you call a body? She poked June again in the stomach with her walking stick of a snake.

June looked into the Witch Doctor's eyes and nodded gently.

Very well, the Witch Doctor said. The first thing we will need then is an elephant.

With her options long exhausted, June had little choice but to consent to the Witch Doctor's unorthodox treatment. The gang of doctors, however, were acting mostly out of curiosity and, possibly, from the guilt they felt about their own endlessly ineffective remedies. They agreed to assist the Witch Doctor in whatever way possible and promptly set out to fill her meticulous orders.

With the help of June's mother, half of the doctors tracked down as many of June's relatives as they could. The other half of the doctors made their way to the local zoo where they begged, cajoled and finally bribed the zoo's staff to lend them their largest elephant, Kingsford, for the day.

The next morning, the Witch Doctor addressed the crowd of relatives, doctors and any other curious staff members who had gathered in the sunny courtyard nestled on the hospital's rooftop.

The string is of the sea, the Witch Doctor said aloud, and as such it must be returned to the sea. In order for us to accomplish this, we must stretch the string out to its absolute limit. Now, this will require an enormous feat of strength and dedication. Make no mistake, this is no easy task, and its end result is far from certain. Anyone fearful of risk and danger should leave now.

The only person to turn and leave upon hearing the Witch Doctor's warning was a janitor who had worked at the hospital for years and was mere weeks away from retirement; he felt he had seen enough uncertainty to last him a lifetime.

The Witch Doctor then went on to explain her plan in full, and once she was finished the crowd leapt to follow her instructions. The doctors secured June to her hospital bed and then secured the bed with locks and chains to the cold concrete of the hospital itself. The Witch Doctor then fed the string off of the roof to the crowd of June's relatives, doctors and various onlookers who had gathered in the street below. Milton Moses Morrison himself was there to pick the string's end out of the air and tie it around the great neck of Kingsford who was happily rubbing his great gray flank against a sedan which had unluckily parked in the street that day.

Led by Milton Moses Morrison riding atop Kingsford, the crowd then marched south through the black streets for miles and miles as they slowly made their way to the white beaches and green waters of the nearby sea. Strung aloft behind them all the while was the slack crystal string streaming out of June's ear. As the crowd continued on, more and more people left their houses to join their ranks, each attracted, no doubt, by Kingsford's bellows, and pretty soon dozens upon dozens of chattering faces had been added to the merry parade.

Once they came within sight of the ocean's roaring green mouth, the string suddenly went taut and tightened with a sharp twang. The doctors and June's relatives then grabbed onto the string and began to pull it toward the gurgling green waves crashing behind them. Each member of the crowd joined in also and soon hundreds of hands were pulling on the string with the gusto of a great game of Tug-of-War. Inch by inch, they labored behind the elephant against the taut crystal string until they could feel the salty breath of the ocean on the backs of their necks.

Atop the hospital, June's tilted head grimaced from the extreme pressure. Her mother held onto her hand, and the cousins who had remained behind offered her whatever words of encouragement they could think of.

Hang in there, they said. You're doing great. Stay strong. The Witch Doctor, meanwhile, said nothing and merely peered through a telescope towards the sea.

When she finally saw Kingsford reach the water's edge, she turned to June's mother and cousins and told them to begin pulling on the string, too. They did as they were told and minutes later, the string began to tremble and vibrate. The Witch Doctor watched on tensely as the very air itself seemed to hum.

Keep pulling, the old woman urged.

June then suddenly cried out loud and the string broke free from her head. A great pop echoed over the town like a loud cannon shot and June's mother and cousins were very nearly thrown off the top of the hospital. Down by the beach, the string fell slack, sending Kingsford and the entire crowd hurtling into the breaking waves of the ocean.

When June's mother got back unto her feet, she held up the loose string and attached to its end, she found a common red rubber stopper, like one would use to plug up the drain of a sink.

We did it, she said triumphantly We did it! She rushed to embrace June, who was staring forward in an empty daze. June's mother hugged her close and when she let go to thank the Witch Doctor, she felt a wetness spreading across the front of her blouse. She looked up at June and saw a gush of tears pouring forth from the girl's green eyes.

June, her mother said, why are you crying?

I don't know, June said, frightened. She didn't know because, in reality, she wasn't crying at all, but was instead leaking. Little by little, water soon began to trickle out of her ears, dribble from the corners of her mouth, and even spray forth from her nose in two great torrents. It leaked off of the bed and began to gather into deep crystal pools on the concrete floor. One of June's cousins dipped her finger in one of the puddles and touched the sparkling liquid to her tongue.

Saltwater, the girl said with a confused scowl.

Saltwater? the Witch Doctor repeated. You mean like seawater?

Instead of waiting for an answer, though, the Witch Doctor rushed for a nearby fire escape.

Save yourselves while you can! she called over her shoulder. The last anyone heard of her was the sound of her crocodile shoes clopping as she vanished down the metal stairs.

Unfortunately for June's mother and her cousins, they did not heed the old woman's advice and remained watching as more and more seawater gushed from June's body in greater and greater streams. They all watched, enthralled, as June's arms began to quake and jitter as if she were being electrocuted and then, suddenly, a huge surge of glittering water burst forth from the girl's mouth and swept her relatives from the courtyard in a great winding river.

By the time the parade of relatives, doctors, and onlookers made their way back to the hospital, each expecting to be greeted as heroes, they found great waterfalls of shimmering seawater pouring out of every window of the hospital into the street below.

My god! said Milton Moses Morrison, still perched atop Kingsford. The girl had a goddamn tsunami inside of her!

The cascade continued for eleven straight days, flooding the town and transforming the streets into salty channels of sparkling water. Fish, crab and curious porpoises swam casually in and out of homes. Sharks picked off house pets. And the screeching chorus of gulls could be heard at all hours of the day.

The townspeople were so overwhelmed by the damage done to their town, fending off jellyfish and electric eels, they had forgotten entirely where the offending waters had originated from in the first place.

Thankfully, on the eleventh day, fate relented and the tide swept the waters out to sea, leaving the town miraculously dry again. Despite the ruin all around them, the townspeople marveled at how lovely the sparkle of salt made their streets and buildings. They now lived in what felt like a town cast of diamonds.

This did little, however, to sate their anger, and with the hospital now accessible, Milton Moses Morrison himself assembled a mob of doctors and angry homeowners, each armed with fishing gaffes and spear guns they had used to fend off sharks, lobsters and flocks of cunning gulls, and the group made their way back to the rooftop of the hospital.

Expecting to find June in the courtyard, they were surprised to find the poor girl's mother instead, and in her arms wasn't her daughter, but an unconscious young boy, naked to the bottoms of his feet. June's mother looked up at the mob of people and in her eyes they saw she was crying. Regular tears, though, thankfully.

It's my son, said June's mother. I thought I had lost him forever, but he's come back to me. My precious, beautiful son.

The mob stood and watched in silence as the mother cradled her previously lost child as if he were still a baby, until one by one, the crowd broke off, and they each returned to their homes to sweep away the piles of clams, jellyfish and dried mounds of dead fish left over from the flood.

No one ever did see June again. Rumors passed about the town that her ghost wandered the pier late at night whenever there was a full moon. Some sleepy-eyed fishermen even claimed to have spotted the girl swimming in the bay during the early morning hours. Most of these rumors, though, were little more than idle talk and eventually they, too, were swallowed up by more interesting gossip washing through the town.

Occasionally, though, whenever a violent storm swept over the town and flooded the streets, anyone who listened closely could indeed hear young June's voice singing softly behind the howls of wind, or ringing up from the rippling puddles dancing along with the endless rush of rain.

© 2016 Anthony Johnson

About the Author: Anthony has an MFA in Creative Writing from the University of Washington and is currently writing a cycle of science fiction stories. He can be reached on Twitter at @adjohnexpers.

"Blood"

by Helia S. Rethmann

Heather had just raised her arm, when the alarm let out three shrill rings, which meant the place was on lockdown. Too late. Too late. And it was her own fault.

"Not again," Shona's book slammed shut. "Why is this always happening right before lunch?"

Kyle, who was charged with in-class security, bolted the door.

"Leave se books open, please," Frau Schrampf said. 'sis will gif us more time to finish se story."

Demetrius and a few others got up and peered out the bulletproof windows. "Can't see nothin'," Demetrius said. Can't hear nothing, neither."

"Setzen!" Frau Schrampf used the Moot Court gavel to pound her desk. "Sofort setzen! If you do not sit down at once you vill get a demerit."

The boys and Carla—who was always with them—returned to their desks.

"This story is really boring," Carla said, flipping pages. "The sentences are, like, a mile long."

"By the time I get to the end of one I've forgotten the beginning," LaTasha said.

"Böll is very dense, yes," Frau Schrampf conceded. But to those who have patience he vill reveal layer and layer of meaning."

Kyle looked at his watch and said: "Ten more minutes to surrender."

The tension headache this morning should have alerted her, Heather thought. She should have stayed home or at least brought something, but she hadn't, and now her future looked dismal.

"I'm starving," Shona said. Can those of us who've brought stuff eat it now?"

Frau Schrampf shook her head. 've vill vait a vhile," she said, and Shona laid down her head and fake-wept theatrically. Heather raised her arm once more.

"May I please be excused, Frau Schrampf? Darf ich bitte, bitte austreten? Es ist ein NOTFALL."

"Sorry, Kind,"Frau Schrampf said. "You know ve can't make exceptions. You vill have to holt it." Holding it, Heather knew, wasn't an option. Already she could feel the warm spot spreading and staining her light-colored pants. She was afraid to look.

They heard screams then, but it was hard to tell if the screams were conveying terror or animation, as they were followed by hysterical laughter.

"Here come the pigs!" Demetrius announced, and his group rushed back to the windows. Strobe lights blazed from four cop cars and three fire engines.

"Check! It! Out!" Carla said. Officers in riot gear were dispersing to and through the main entrances and around the buildings.

"I bet one of your brothers brought his invention to school," Owen said to Nadim, who was Muslim.

"So not funny," LaTasha said.

"Shame on you!" Frau Schrampf pointed her gavel at Owen. "For sat you vill get a demerit."

Kyle said, "Three more minutes."

"It was a joke." Owen looked around but nobody felt like backing him up. "Me and the man are, like, best buds forever!" Nadim shook his head, without raising his eyes from his well-worn German book.

"Sat is a very sat sense of humor, young man," Frau Schrampf said, looking straight at Owen. Owen blushed. Heather, who'd once had a thing for Owen, sat motionless and prayed. Dear Lord or Lady: I know I'm of no importance to you. But if it's all the same, make Owen say more stupid things so everyone will look at him and nobody will look at me. Make a fight break out. Make the walls cave in and the ceiling come down. Give Frau Schrampf a medical emergency. No. No—don't do that. Don't take her, but kill me. Quickly and without much pain. If you'll do that I will, I will—

"Time. Please surrender your personal weapons," Kyle said.

The class groaned. They searched their backpacks and patted down their bodies, and, one by one, they walked over to where Kyle stood and deposited their handguns into the steel basket he was holding out to them and signed their names on his clipboard.

"Thank you," Kyle said to each one of them.

"This rule makes no sense," La Tasha said, dropping her 8 mm Luger, and Kyle said: "Rule number three: After fifteen minutes of any in-class lockdown situation—"

"Yeah, whatever," LaTasha said, cutting him off.

"Thank you," Kyle said.

Shona had trouble detaching her sparkling holster from her belt, and when she finally did, there were gasps of envy.

"Valentine's gift from my man," Shona said. The studs looked like real diamonds.

"Pretty," LaTasha said. Carla said,

"Check. It. Out."

Now, Heather was the only one left in her seat. She smiled at Frau Schrampf, willing her brain to convey an emergency message.

"Heather, Kind, ve do neet you to comply wis school policy," Frau Schrampf said. Heather stood up, and almost immediately Demetrius screamed: "Look! Heather's been shot! She's bleeding!"

And everyone looked before averting their eyes, and Heather thought how peaceful it would be, to be actually dead.

©2016 Helia S. Rethmann

About the Author: Helia grew up in Germany, but now lives in Nashville, Tennessee, where she teaches, writes, and cleans up after too many animals. Her fiction has recently appeared in Black Elephant, Intrinsick Magazine and in Pure Slush and Virgins anthologies. Her story "Animals" was published recently by the Breakwater Review (U of MA at Boston), and "The truth about the children you rooted for" will be included in the "Fairy Tales and Folklore Re-imagined" anthology by "Between-the-Lines" this September.

"A Practiced Office Dance"

by Tarsilla Moura

Jillian Montgomery climbed the steps to her office on the 4th floor. Her high heels sounded loud in the silent stairwell. It was 8:47 AM, and already she tugged at her blazer restlessly. The day hadn't even begun, and yet she felt drained. Boxed in. Usually avoiding the building's invasively crowded elevators helped, but today not even taking the stairs worked.

She entered her office floor, head held high but eyes never resting on anyone for long. Making herself small and invisible, that had always been Jill's formula to a good day when she was younger. But she quickly learned she couldn't stay invisible forever. Before long, what had kept her sheltered from the world had suddenly made her easy pickings. A target.

She now knew not to stare at the floor like her instincts always screamed at her to do. Instead she learned new tricks: Give off the impression of confidence without inviting challenge; Look up but never make eye contact; Don't hide sweaty palms or shy away from contact; shake someone's hand firmly but never for long.

"Good morning, Jill," she heard a deep, male voice too close to her ear.

"Morning, beautiful day, isn't it?" she answered. She never stopped walking until she reached her cubicle. It was no longer about invisibility. She was a master of deception now.

"Jill! You're early," someone else said. He leaned against the grey foam partition, obstructing the way out. She registered his presence but turned her back to him.

"Yep. Had an early start today," she said. She never faltered in removing her blazer, stashing her briefcase, and turning on her monitor. Be friendly but look busy. Don't look bothered or put out.

"Any plans for Thanksgiving?" he asked, still in her space. She vaguely recognized him. She wasn't sure. She never looked long enough to know what any of them looked like. She sat in her chair and tucked herself closer against her desk. She threw a distracted smile over her shoulder.

"Going back home, spending it with family."

People are used to being half-ignored, she's found. People no longer expect someone's full attention. She's learned to use that to her advantage.

"Can you believe I completely forgot to turn in the survey results over the weekend?" Jill threw another practiced look and hair toss over her shoulder. "My head, I swear. Good thing I'm early."

From the corner of her eye she saw him falter and take a step back. Already she could breathe more easily.

"Better let you get on that," he said.

"Gotta get it done," she laughed. He finally walked away. She suppressed a relieved sigh.

She stayed in her cubicle for the remainder of the morning. When lunch came around, she waited until everyone was settled in the break room or at their own desks. She then grabbed her salad bowl and moved to the copy room. She usually ate while she did the filing she needed to get done for the day.

The rhythmic, automatic noises of the copier soothed her. She let the motion and sounds of the machine fill her mind while she munched on her quinoa salad. She didn't notice she was no longer alone.

The sound of the paper tray of the adjacent photocopier slamming shut yanked her out of her trance. She shivered so violently she almost dropped her bowl. She turned wide, startled eyes to the new intruder, berating herself for her inattention.

"You alright there, dear?"

"Ms. Hart," she breathed a sigh of relief. It wasn't one of them. It was just Ms. Hart. "You startled me."

"I'm so sorry. This damned thing. Always running out of paper."

Jill looked at Ms. Hart frowning down at the photocopier. The older woman was short and plump, and she sported a full head of white hair. Jill sometimes sought her grandmotherly presence. They were the only two women in the office.

"So," Ms. Hart turned to her. "I heard you tell Lester you were going home for Thanksgiving."

"Yes," Jill meekly answered. She could feel a blush heating up her neck and cheeks. She had told Ms. Hart she would be celebrating with a few friends in town. "Change of plans."

"Right," Ms. Hart said, and Jill could clearly hear the disbelief in her voice.

She hated lying. She was good at it, great even. After years of conditioning herself, the lies just spilled out of her lips. But she still hated doing it, hated that she had to do it. She opened her mouth to explain, to apologize, to confess. She couldn't find the words.

"Well, it's just me and my husband this year. My daughter is overseas and my son and his wife just had a baby." Jill closed her mouth, surprised. "We would love to have you over. It looks like you have plans, but should they fall through… In any case. You're welcome to spend Thanksgiving with us."

Jill was mortified to find sudden tears prick at her eyes. She quickly turned back and looked down at her copier. The machine was still, and the copies sat in the output tray waiting for her. No wonder the silent room was too loud in her head. She racked her brain for words.

A hand on her shoulder brought her out of her inner turmoil.

"Dear, you can either make it or you can't. It's fine either way," Ms. Hart said, careful to extract her hand, Jill noticed. "I'd just hate to see you miss out on Thanksgiving, is all." Jill nodded, honestly too overwhelmed to say anything. Ms. Hart smiled and left the copy room. Before the older woman could get too far, Jill called her back.

"Thank you," she said. "I, just — thank you."

With another smile, Ms. Hart went back to her desk. No longer hungry, Jill threw away the rest of her salad and went back to her cube, fresh batch of copies in hand.

© 2016 Tarsilla Moura

About the Author: Tarsilla is the Managing Editor at *Global HealthCare Insights* magazine. She recently graduated from Emerson College with a Master's degree in Publishing and Writing, and completed her graduate thesis on the applicability of online fanfiction within the publishing industry. She received her Bachelor's degree in English Language & Literature from the University of Maryland, with a focus on creative writing and editing. Tarsilla divides her time between Boston,

Washington D.C. and her home country of Brazil. When not working, she is either tutoring international students on English writing and speaking, reviewing romance novels, or reading and writing fanfiction. Follow her at @tsm_athena.

"Country Club Christmas"

by Michelle Cox

I'm sitting on the bench by the hostess stand of the country club's restaurant, humming along to the song "Grandma Got Run Over by a Reindeer", thinking "Where are the Reindeer when you need them?"

Then Officer Joachim interrupts my tune.

"I'm doing you a big favor," he says, snapping his notebook shut. "Procedure says someone should be leaving here in handcuffs. Merry Christmas."

"Thank you. I appreciate it," I lie, knowing he's extending me this professional courtesy because I work for the prosecutor's office. In truth, I'd love to see my mother in handcuffs.

We always go to the club on Christmas Eve. My mother – the grandma upon whom I am wishing death by reindeer – conjured up this tradition when I was a child because she hated cooking Christmas Eve dinner for my Dad's family. She told my Great Aunt Lorna that in exchange for Aunt Lorna hosting the holiday dinner at the club, we would all attend church with her afterwards.

This marks our 19th Christmas Eve at Worthington Hills Country Club. However, we have never been to church with my aunt.

Tonight, when I arrived at the club with my husband and 3-year-old daughter, Katie, I overheard the woman who would be our waitress talking quietly into her phone. As she talked, I noticed the scarf wrapping her bald head, a telltale sign of chemo treatments.

"Don't worry. Mommy will be home before Santa comes," she said. "Be a good girl and go to bed for Angela. We'll have so much fun tomorrow. Your nana can't wait to see you. Love you baby."

I wrapped my arm around my daughter's shoulders and gave a squeeze as I eavesdropped on the waitress, mentally assessing her situation: single mom trying to support a kid on a waitress' salary while battling cancer, no dad, probably a small apartment. I bet Santa's delivery will be meager compared to the one at my house tonight. I felt sorry for her.

She ended the call and caught me staring. I gave her a sympathetic smile.

"Merry Christmas," I said. "I'm sorry you have to work tonight."

"It's okay," she said smiling. "We have a lot to celebrate and we're doing it tomorrow. We've got big plans to spend the holiday with my folks. We're going to bake cookies all day. We love Christmas."

We were seated for 15 minutes at a long table with my parents, my aunt and brother, and his wife, waiting for my sister's family to arrive. When they hustled in, my mother complained about their tardiness.

"We had a neighborhood party," my sister Janet said. "It's not a big deal."

My mother's lower jaw seemed to unlock from its hinges, moving forward three inches to create a bulldog looking under bite that always spells trouble. She growled something to Janet through clenched teeth, but I couldn't hear because Katie was saying that she needed to "go potty."

Janet got up and stormed away from the table. I watched her angry departure and then looked back at my mother, who threw down her napkin, and stood and left the table in an equally dramatic fashion.

My husband and I were the only ones who noticed this little drama unfolding. We both raised our eyebrows and I shrugged my shoulders.

"Not my circus. Not my monkeys. For once I'm not the one who set Mom off on a holiday," I said.

"I want to go potty," Katie whined again.

"Not right now. Let's order our food first," I said, not wanting to walk Katie into the shit storm that my mother and sister were conjuring in the restroom.

My child took the "no" in stride, climbed off my lap, and wandered down to her relatives at the other end of the table. I turned to my husband.

"I'd love to be a fly on the wall in that bathroom. I wonder how Janet is faring in the ring with Mom. She's not used to being on the receiving end of mom's bullshit," I said.

"I hope they get it resolved before they come back to our house for presents. That tension makes me uncomfortable."

"Get used to it, bucko," I retorted. "Tension, drama, someone – usually me – disappointing Mom by not following the script for the perfect Christmas? That's what holidays in this family are all about."

The waitress arrived at our end of the table with a smile and asked if she could take drink orders. As she ran through the beer list for my husband, my sister-in-law appeared beside me, holding my daughter's hand.

"You're here. Thank God. I assumed it was you fighting with your mom, but I guess it's Janet. Your mom's gonna get arrested," she said breathlessly.

She explained that Katie asked to go to the restroom, but when they got there, the manager had the area blocked off.

"He told me two women were fighting and he had called the cops. Then I heard your mom and sister screaming at each other, and I thought it was you. It sounded like it was getting physical, so I hustled Katie back here." I walked to the other end of the table and whispered in my father's ear.

"Mom's finally done it," I said. "And this time the cops are on their way. This will be a Christmas for the memory books."

I watch the police officer exit the club before turning to head back to the table where my family resumed the festivities. They are eating, pretending for my aunt's sake that everything is fine. I'm not sure what they've told her – probably something about one of us being ill. She's not stupid and knows something is up, but she also knows my mother and understands that it's best to play along to keep the peace.

Before I reach the table, our waitress crosses my path.

"I'm sorry YOU have to work tonight," she says, giving me a sympathetic look.

About the Author: Michelle Cox is a professional freelance writer who got her start as a print reporter. She's a contributor to Mamalode, 5Minutesformom and The Good Men Project, and is a word slinger for a handful of corporate clients – the stuff that pays the bills. She also conducts budget-friendly social media book launch campaigns and is preparing to introduce two unique creative writing courses: one for individuals in recovery and another combining yoga and creative writing (details at writingyourwords. com). Though much of her work is nonfiction, her true love is *truth-telling through fiction*. Regardless of genre, she believes in "the power of a writing to give us authorship of our storyline so we can make peace with time, find joy, quiet fear, euthanize isolation and create a community of common experience." Michelle currently is working on her first novel and has won a few awards/recognitions for her short stories including 2nd place in the Gemini Magazine Flash Fiction Contest (2017) and a finalist in the Atlantis Short Story Contest (2016). Michelle and her husband have three children (ages 23, 20 and 10) and they live in St. Louis, Mo. You can find her at michellecoxwriter.com

"Groundhog Days"

by Conner Russell

1

February 2nd was warm and sunny when the groundhog stuck his head out.

"I'm so alone," Tommy said to the groundhog. The groundhog studied Tommy's river of tears and receded back into his hole.

2

The clouds blocked out the sunrise.

"Mornings without sunrises are portentous," Tommy used to tell me. I didn't want to say that the day Isabelle left him began with the most magnificent sunrise I'd ever seen.

"I wish the groundhogs could see this," Tommy said minutes before Isabelle called to say it was over.

By noon the sky was black and trickles of rain floated toward the ground. By 5 PM, the freeways were gridlocked as tired motorists marveled at the now fully formed raindrops smashing against their motionless windshields.

3

Tommy opened his umbrella and sat near the groundhog's hole.

"Come out," he yelled, but the groundhog had no intention of leaving. He was deep asleep, dreaming of flowers.

4

On February 7th I had a job interview at a home improvement store. They asked me all sorts of questions that at the time seemed irrelevant.

"We have a lot of groundhogs around here; do you know how to deal with them?"

I lied and said yes.

"There's also a sad man that hangs out with them. Do you know how to deal with sad men?" I almost said the sad man was my good friend Tommy but instead I said:

"I've dealt with a few in my time."

The interviewer posited a situation:

"Say you're at the register and a groundhog comes in looking for flowers. What do you do?" It felt like a trap.

"I'd ask the groundhog if they needed assistance then discreetly call the manager."

"Thank you for your time."

5

Tommy, after a slow walk around the park, was feeling better about his devastating loss when the groundhog emerged.

"Why have you been ignoring me?" Tommy asked.

"Everyone ignores everyone," the groundhog replied. "Get out of my way, I need to find something to eat." February 15th, like the 26 days before it, ended in tears for Tommy.

6

The interviewer called on the 18th and said I got the job. I was to start immediately, as they were shorthanded on cashiers after a few had been fired for letting groundhogs abscond with flowers.

When I got there, I was handed a fluorescent apron weighed down by buttons demonstrating my lack of knowledge: "I'M IN TRAINING", or my lack or agency "ASK ME ABOUT OUR CREDIT CARD", or my lack of a belief system "WHEEL OF VAL-UES". Then I was sentenced to retrieve shopping carts from the parking lot.

"People are afraid of the groundhogs so they're leaving their shopping carts out there," my interviewer said. "Go get "em." Fear makes people do irrational things. Like yell and fight and leave their shopping carts in parking lots. I watched as a woman shoved her cart into the side of a truck.

"There's no time for decency anymore," she yelled, "not with all these groundhogs running around."

I saw only a handful of groundhogs on my cart runs. They lounged in the dirt eating soggy brown grass, bullshitting with bored squirrels and pigeons. On the periphery of their group was Tommy, nervously writing love letters to Isabelle. He locked eyes on me and rushed over.

"My letter starts: Isabelle, I know change is hard to come by in this day and age, but if there's anyone who can change, it's me: you know that! How much did we change together? How we changed in such beautiful ways. You, from a—"

"I have to get more carts," I cut him off. He crumpled like the leaves of a dandelion in the mouth of a big groundhog.

7

Tommy's letter went through multiple drafts.

Isabelle, I know change is hard to come by, but if there's a single person who could do it

Isabelle, change is a difficult thing, but it doesn't always have to be

Isabelle, we all want change and don't want change at the same time. Change is paralyzing us... me.

"Terrible," said the groundhog as he retired to his hole for the evening.

8

They still had me pushing carts around on March 1. My co-worker Jon made me a modified Wheel of Values, one I couldn't attach to my apron. It was called "The Wheel of No Diploma," divided into seven equal parts:

- FAST FOOD CASHIER

- CONSTRUCTION CLEAN-UP CREW

- COSMETOLOGIST

- PARTY CLOWN

- JANITOR

- GROUNDHOG

- LOT ASSOCIATE

I told him I knew people with diplomas who did all those things and he rescinded his Wheel of No Diploma and cried and cried and...

9

Tommy's first smile came on March 2nd. The groundhog basked in a tiny sliver of sunlight while disenfranchised hawks sized him up.

"Shouldn't you be hiding?" Tommy asked.

"What's the point?" the groundhog said. "I've got nothing on these bones." The hawks must have realized this because they sighed heavily and flew away.

Tommy smiled. "You're so wise"

"I forgot you were still here," the groundhog said.

10

I have resigned from my position at the home improvement store. Here's what happened:

I was told I needed to convince people to sign up for credit cards. As a joke, I asked Tommy if he was interested and to my surprise he said yes. He needed financing to buy a bunch of shovels so he could dig a hole and live with the groundhogs.

Predictably, he was declined and my supervisor got a sour look and said: "Get real people to sign up."

Then I found an old man and told him how great and altruistic the store was to extend him such an amazing offer.

"What's the APR?" he asked.

"Multiply the number of groundhogs out in the parking lot by two," I said. Riotous laughter fell out of his mouth and off he went.

As I turned around Tommy was walking off with two shovels.

"Did you pay for those?" I asked.

"No," Tommy said.

My supervisor told me to stop him at once. Instead, I gently placed my apron in the trash can and followed Tommy. February 18th to March 15th, not a particularly impressive career.

11

Tommy and the narrator spent all of March 16th digging a hole. They took their time and really made it something to be proud of. Tommy added windows into the tunnels so he could wave as the groundhogs scurried past. He added a bathroom where he could take mud baths. He added a living room with a clay futon. And in his bedroom was a bed of grass and thousands of half-written letters.

Later, Tommy and the narrator burned those letters while sitting around a campfire with the groundhogs.

"So what if you're alone and ignored," the groundhog said wisely. "You've got a hole to call your own and that's worth something."

The next day the clouds disappeared and the flowers came out. It wasn't winter anymore.

About the Author: Conner is from San Diego and is currently studying English and Creative Writing at the University of California, Berkeley. He is at work on short stories, essays for class, and a novel loosely based on his experiences hitchhiking and train-hopping around the country.

"Ambition"

by Michael Colonnese

"Did this in Caesar seem ambitious?
When that the poor have cried, Caesar hath wept.
Ambition should be made of sterner stuff."

– Shakespeare

Marty McGrath, Leo Fisher's 10th grade English teacher, was clearly upset when the boy refused to read Julius Caesar aloud in Special Ed. Instead, Leo sat in the back of McGrath's classroom, surrounded by a pile of musty-smelling philosophy texts and short-story collections, discards from the public library, while the only other three students who were able to read at all were expected to soldier on—with or without Leo's participation. There was Ruby Toomer, a Downs-Syndrome black girl who liked to listen to top forty and play patty-cake, and whose stepfather had removed her front teeth with a pair of pliers to improve the quality of her blowjobs. There was Lucy

Fernandez, potentially bilingual and one of the so-called 'dreamers", but who had to be watched carefully for any signs of emotional stress that might signal the onset of debilitating seizures. Lastly there was Leo's best buddy, Tommy Albright, who had a heart defect and webbed fingers. Tommy probably didn't belong in Special Ed classes either but was unusually compliant and agreeable.

The rest of the Special Ed students were simply hopeless, slack-jawed, pimply faced, and indistinguishable in their hopelessness except that some of them smelled fecal, wore diapers, and sat in wheelchairs. Once Leo had demonstrated that he could already read and write, most of his teachers had decided to leave him alone, but when McGrath dared imagine that a student attracted to old books might possibly be interested in Shakespeare, Leo had responded with a vacant stare. It was the boy's deliberate indifference that galled. It was bad enough that his other students were droolers—as nearly everyone in administration secretly called them—but to have a Special Ed kid who showed real ability but wouldn't perform, well, that rankled. McGrath had tried explaining to Leo that, even if he stuck things out for the full four years, a Special Ed certificate wasn't nearly as valuable as a diploma, but the boy seemed determined to quit attending high-school as soon as he turned sixteen, and insisted that it didn't matter where test scores had misplaced him.

If McGrath had been a novice instructor, he would likely have taken Leo's pending decision to become a dropout personally; the soon-to-be-wasted human potential might have driven him out of teaching, but McGrath was a twenty-five-year veteran. He had a state pension waiting if he decided to retire, and it was entirely by choice that he taught a class of droolers. He had seniority, and if he'd wanted to pull rank, he could have taught nothing but Advanced Placement classes or the gifted and talented. Instead, every year he elected to teach a section of

Special Ed—primarily as an example for the younger instructors, but also to prove he could still survive in the trenches.

"That goddamn kid doesn't want to be saved," McGrath announced to those gathered in the shabby faculty lounge during lunch break. Nearly a dozen teachers were occupying mismatched couches and arm chairs, and a few more huddled around a splattered and grungy microwave, where a Lean-Cuisine entrée revolved. None of them even bothered to nod. Instead, they looked down at the threadbare carpet, or out through latticed-steel windows at the steel gray sky that hung like a pall over downtown Detroit. It was March 15th, nearly spring, but winter wasn't over yet, and expressing anger about an untenable situation wasn't helpful. Besides, nearly all of them had experienced their own frustrating interactions with Leo Fisher, or had heard McGrath complain bitterly about the boy before, so they already knew exactly which goddamn kid he meant.

"So, screw Leo Fisher," said Martha Lemmings. "Save the ones you can." As the only guidance counselor at Warren Harding High, where nine of every ten students received free or reduced-cost lunches, Mrs. Lemmings was singlehandedly responsible for arranging twelve-hundred student schedules and encouraging college applications from a handful of optimistic over-achievers who imagined they had futures, but also for meeting with the parents or guardians of students who had gotten pregnant or into fist fights, or else had been caught carrying knives, drugs, or handguns and faced mandatory expulsion.

Martha had known McGrath for fifteen years, and they'd once had a brief sexual fling, a one night's stand, which both subsequently blamed on hard apple cider consumed at a faculty Christmas party, but that was many years ago. Martha had since married a muscular gym teacher named Lemmings, who fortunately no longer worked at the same school. McGrath and his wife, Margie, had been invited to their wedding, but he had felt awkward, claimed he'd had previous engagement, sent a small gift, but didn't attend. Nowadays, McGrath's sex life was non-existent. Two years ago, his wife, Margie, had suffered a debilitating stroke and needed private nursing care when he was away at work.

"I wonder what his home life is like," McGrath muttered. He was no longer speaking to Mrs. Lemmings so much as to himself, and was taken back when she responded with something like compassion.

"It's often better not to pry."

"You're his guidance counselor," McGrath said, "Isn't that your job?" If he couldn't get a response from Leo, he could always guilt-trip Mrs. Lemmings.

"If you had to listen to half the twisted stories I vet on a daily basis, you'd appreciate the students who fail to communicate."

"I simply expected him to read a few lines from Julius Caesar," McGrath said.

"Beware the ides of March," said Mrs. Lemming, "Isn't that in there somewhere?"

McGrath shrugged. "No doubt," he said, excusing himself before the period bell. He headed for an empty student lavatory, where while studying himself in the unbreakable steel mirror that hung above the sink, he wept as he washed his hands.

©2017 Michael Colonnese

About the Author: Michael Colonnese lives in Fayetteville, NC where he directs the Creative Writing Program at Methodist University and works as the Managing Editor of Longleaf Press. His fiction and poetry books are available on Amazon. com. His latest is a poetry collection entitled Double Feature.

"Berserk"

by Bob Joncas

The day that Lisa Crenshaw walked into Bea's Antique and Curio Shop, the last thing on her mind was murder. Lisa slowly walked through the store, perusing each item. Rounding a corner of cluttered shelves, an unusual cast iron muffin pan caught her eye. It sat on the back of a shelf surrounded by objects once used by nameless people—certainly long dead.

The intricate pan held a mold of eight bears—all different and unique. The handles were scrolled and ornate. She rushed to the front of the store and waved her credit card in front of an elderly woman, anxious to pay for her prize.

Lisa felt giddy as she climbed inside the car. She drove straight home and rushed into her apartment. She unpacked the pan and noticed that there were small patches of rust. She got out a brush and cleaned off the rust. She whipped up a cornbread recipe, poured batter into each of the eight bear forms, and put the pan in the oven.

Lisa went to put on her nightgown and noticed in the mirror that her unruly hair could use a trip to the hairdresser. She cut her own hair and bought her clothes at the thrift store. She didn't feel worthy of new clothes and expensive salons.

The phone rang, and Lisa flinched, that would be her mother. Lisa let the phone go on ringing. God, why couldn't her mother just leave her alone!

Her father walked out on Lisa and her younger brother, Brian, when she was ten. Her alcoholic mother was the reason they constantly moved. Lisa and her brother never stayed in one place long enough to make friends. Brian inherited Mother's bad traits. His addiction to drugs and alcohol eventually killed him.

She went to the kitchen and opened the oven door, pulling out the rack where eight little golden-brown bears simmered in the pan. The sweet cornbread aroma permeated the room. Lisa took out a jar of honey, waiting for the muffins to cool…gazing at the pan.

Lisa carefully removed each bear from the pan and laid them out on a platter. Out of the pan, the difference in the bear molds was even more evident. One bear had its arms crossed over its chest, another its legs bent up to the stomach. One had two hands over its mouth—speak no evil—the other, its hands over both ears—hear no evil—another with two hands over its eyes—see no evil.

Lisa trembled.

Frightened, she turned her attention to the five other bear muffins. They were also posed in different directions, one with its eyes closed, the other four with their eyes wide open. Animal molds were usually whimsical, not serious and surreal. A cold shiver ran down her spine.

Lisa carried the plate with the two bears to the table beside her chair and placed it next to the book she was reading. She picked up the book, and absently reached for a honey covered bear. She brought it to her lips and bit into the delicious morsel—and before she knew it—the two scrumptious bears had disappeared.

A loud crash startled Lisa and she jumped up off the chair. Her heart pounded as she raced into the kitchen. The bear pan had fallen onto the floor. Lisa picked the pan up off the floor and laid it on the counter. Feeling apprehensive, Lisa went back to the chair and picked up her book.

As she started reading, Lisa felt her stomach lurch. She rubbed her belly to soothe it and decided to get something from the medicine cabinet. She started coughing so hard that her ribs were burning. She tried to get out of the chair, but the fits were so severe that she became paralyzed. She couldn't catch her breath. "Oh no!" Lisa rolled to her side in the chair gasping for a breath. Her body violently shuddered with spasms. Her lungs were on fire. She felt like something had crawled up inside her windpipe and blocked it. If she didn't get help soon, she was going to die.

"BAM-BAM-BAM!!!" She rolled her head to the side, and through blurry eyes, focused on the platter sitting on the kitchen counter. The six remaining bears on the plate were standing up hunched over, facing her and screaming, "YOU ATE OUR BROTHERS! YOU ATE OUR BROTHERS! THEY ARE DEAD—AND NOW—YOU ARE DEAD!!!" Over and over—until she slipped into unconsciousness…

Lisa opened her eyes to a bright light. Her throat was raw. She slowly turned her head and looked into her mother's stern face.

"What happened?" Lisa moaned.

"I drove over to your apartment when you didn't answer the phone. I knew you weren't on a date, or with friends, since you don't have any. I pounded on the door and heard odd noises inside. I went to find the apartment manager, and he opened the door with his key. We found you unconscious. The manager gave you CPR while I called 911. Do you know what you put me through?" her mother screamed.

The next day, Lisa was discharged from the hospital. When she got home, she looked around the apartment at the carnage left from the night before. Did she really see the bears taunting her...or was it her imagination from the lack of oxygen in her brain?

The bear muffins were all over the counter. She picked up the pan to take to the sink and stopped short. There were six molds in the pan, but she knew that there were eight molds when she bought the pan—the rust was back—that's odd. Lisa examined the remaining bears sprawled out on the counter. Six on the counter and the two she ate made eight!

The next morning, Lisa paid her mother a visit. Her mother was surprised.

"Well, you have finally come to your senses, and decided to visit your poor mother!"

"That's right mother, I've come to my senses, and from now on, things will be different between us." Lisa said, handing her mother a plate of six frosted bears.

"This is for all your help. I hope you enjoy them Mother, I have to go." She turned and walked to her car.

As Lisa drove away, she glanced into the rear-view mirror, turning off her cell phone without any sense of remorse. She eyed the muffin pan sitting in the passenger seat, then quickly looked away. She went about her errands to the grocery store, and to get her hair done at Trudy's Salon.

Lisa walked out of Trudy's with an air of confidence, looking stunning, with a new cut and color. She slid in the car and glanced over at the pan on the seat, noticing that only four bear molds remained. Mother must have eaten her gift. Lisa wasn't sorry for what she did. After all, her mother had killed Brian, as surely as if she murdered him in cold blood.

About the Author: Bob is a Real Estate Broker in Munds Park, a small mountain town near Flagstaff, AZ. He has a BS degree and is a graduate of UCLA's Writers Program. Among his many English classes, he has taken Vampires in Literature and Zombies in Literature. He is a member of the Horror Writers Association and is currently working on his novel, "Changing Tide."

"EGG"

by Mary Finnegan

I know to just walk into the cabin in the overgrown forest; there is no lock, no security system. Lit by elongated spherical candles, the expansive room is filled with shadow and stark illumination and eggs.

The ghosts of my ancestors haunt me about what I am about to do. Well, somebody has to put Ma into a nursing home, for her own good. And it should be someone who loves her.

I feel stupid dressed in a suit and tie. Compared to her, I'm big and powerful. And really, I'm not. Inside, I'm still the child who grew up here.

So many children—so many names—we called each other Brother and Sister. Now we have all adopted identities in society. Ma is all alone.

I never had the sense of her being my real mother.... Ma is too old, for one thing. My father? Who knows? Not one of us knows who we belong to. We just belong to one another, us Erie.

She looks at me with eyes so piecing. I wonder if she has gone blind; she looks right through me.

"Ma." That is what the Tribe calls her. Like her Ma and her Ma before her, she is Matriarch of the Erie. Mother to us all. She connects all Erie. And everyone is Erie. Ma claims that a property of the individual Erie is that every Erie contains the complete Tribe.

Ma reflects the whole damn Erie in mirror imagine.

She rocks slowly back and forth in her bouncy chair next to the fire. An Indian blanket covers her hunched back and mane of silver curls. Ma has never cut her hair: she claims it is an extension of the nervous system and enhances her psychic abilities. Eerie, the black cat is curled on her lap, Bloody Stump, the three-legged dog is at her side, and Who? the owl is on her shoulder.

Ma is surrounded by her collection of eggs, perfectly balanced eggs, arranged on antique tables and deep shelves, hanging from the ceiling and stuck to the walls, all different colors and sizes. Jeweled Fabergé eggs are scattered randomly with plastic Easter eggs filled with sweets and small prizes.

And each egg has a story about how she attained it.

There is a crystal egg, given to her by a fortune teller; a black magic-eight egg, that now I hold tight in both sweaty hands. If I turn the magic ball upside down, there is a window that gives an answer. I cannot allow myself a question, such as, am I doing the right thing? I cannot leave my actions up to whimsy.

The eight-ball egg is the only object that survived a fire that burned the barn to the ground and when it was found in the ashes, it read, yes.

On the fireplace mantel, a string of silver eggs, left to Ma by a Wizard, swings back and forth on strings due to their own volition,

And her favorite, an egg the size of a baseball full of floating mirrors, purple liquid and glitter.

I gave her that egg.

I was 13; and I got this feeling, like I was NOW. Purposely I hiked to Erie Eternal Flame Waterfalls. The grotto at the bottom of the 100 foot falls has several fissures through which methane gas is lit. I stood at the center of the whirlpool nearly invisible in the haze of mist blown up from the torrent of the Mad River, which runs both ways. In anticipation, I held out my cupped hands as the mirrored ovum, the size of an invisibubble, tumbled over the vertical drop and I caught it.

Nothing since has ever felt so good, as placing that egg in Ma's hands.

"Where's your medical alert necklace?" I ask. In a silly response, she blows me a kiss with her deformed right hand.

"Do you want some tea?" I ask.

I make us both a cup, like old times, and settle across from her on the settee. The soft light and warmth from the fire is comforting as a womb; I loosen my tie and kick off my shoes.

"How is Who?" I ask, referring to the snow owl on her shoulder. Who? blinks at me with round golden eyes as if she knows what I'm saying.

"She still hasn't flown," Ma says, then adds in a voice held steady, "Who? laid a cuckoo bird's egg that is about to hatch.

I give a strained smile. "Really?"

I sip my herbal tea prepared from the cured leaves of the pot plant. I'd forgotten the warm rush of energy from Erie tea, the feeling of euphoria, and the sublime connection with all things.

"I wrapped the egg in your shit," Ma says, nodding her head that suddenly seems too big for her tiny body.

That statement slams me back to my reason for coming here. Another gulp of tea.

"Ma..."

"Remember, months ago, the last night you spent here? I collected your shit."

This cabin has no plumbing, and I'd had my bowel movement in the outhouse. "Ma, you can't live like this anymore..."

"You had a dream about a beautiful woman. A wet dream. You ejaculated your sperm..."

I feel an impenetrable darkness. "Listen to me, Ma..."

"I collected it."

"You got my shit? You got my sperm?" I hear myself, but can't stop; I am an idiot to converse with her. I know she is suffering from dementia. She needs to be put into an institution where she can be cared for, poor dear.

Ma giggles insanely, "I poked a tiny hole into the egg Who? laid, and injected your semen, after which I sealed the egg's opening with my virgin hymen, which I saved for 70 years. Since the first day of the spring lunar cycle, the equinox— April Fools Day— when eggs can be balanced on end, your shit has incubated the embryo insemi-nated with your sperm."

In a way, I'm glad she's finally gone completely balmy. I've spent a lifetime with magic and superstition and illogical decrees from this old woman. I'm grateful to her for everything. All the love. All the sacrifices. But I want a life! I've spent years being responsible for her and her animals and her cabin and her eggs.

"It's right there, next to the mandrake root!" She points.

On the fireplace hearth is a human-looking root, and next to it a turd shaped like an egg and steaming.

I'm totally discombobulated; I grab Eerie from her lap and clutch the black cat to my heart to hold her tight, as if this small animal can keep me safe in reality. I breathe, hard, and that is all I am capable of.

"It's hatching," Ma says, as Bloody Stump goes to sniff it. I know logically that if I respond to her, I've lost any hope of rescuing Ma, and she needs rescuing— she's insane. A part of me has always known, the poor woman is not in touch with reality. As if from a distance, I hear my own quivering voice. "What's inside the egg?"

"A tiny living humanoid," Ma says.

At first, I think that a sprout is emerging from the egg created from shit. Then I realize it is a tiny arm and hand with delicate fingers grasping the air.

Ma says, "You must feed it sperm from your penis."

A bulbous head covered in slime thick as egg-white emerges through the cracked shell and gives a banshee wail that mingles with my own inhuman lament.

"It looks like you," Ma says proudly.

THE END

About the Author: Mary is Matriarch of the Erie, a tribe notorious for intense psychic abilities. She says she has a disposition for difficulty with authority. Her FB page is THE ERIE IS COMING. She adds, "I live on the dead end of Erie St. with my grandson, Jacob Stump, my owl, Who? my black cat Eerie and my thee-legged dog, Bloody Stump."

"The Woman Who Loved a Spy"

by Leslie Muzingo

April was looking for a rosebush on the easterly section of the hiking trail, to verify the note she'd received was genuine. She found none. If this were a safe place, I'd find a rose somewhere. At least a rose bush.

Stephen always told her to beware of false messages. It was one of the hazards of being in love with a spy. "You must understand the risks," he'd say in that delightful Irish accent of his.

April sighed. She loved thinking about Stephen, the way he talked, walked, even the way he smelled! But now she had to find the rose or leave. That was the rule.

Stephen's work was very dangerous. He never said what agency employed him. Sometimes he couldn't say where he was going or when he'd return. "If I come back," he'd say as she swam in his Irish green eyes.

The message had been pushed under her door but addressed to them both. Stephen wasn't home, so she opened it alone. It said, "the usual clues would be present to assure them of their safety", and to "hurry, a matter of life or death."

There was no rosebush. After teaching all day she was tired, and besides, if she turned west she could see the sunset. There was no danger, just an old car battery by a tree. Something about that bothered her, but the beauty of the view captured her thoughts.

She sat on the ground and worshiped the setting sun. Her thoughts wandered from the missing rose bush to how she first met Stephen.

"How can I help you?" April had asked, thinking this incredibly handsome man must be the father of a student who was about to enter her class.

"I can't explain, but can you tell me the name of Laura Ingalls Wilder's daughter?" This question seemed absurd coming out in an Irish brogue. Once April's giggles were under control, she replied, "Her name was Rose."

Stephen had leaned forward till he was almost a kiss away. "And your name?"

April's throat went dry.

"Please."

"April," she whispered.

"A fine name. The name of a rose with cheeks as pink as yours."

She had smiled at him. "The April Rose is actually a pinkish-orangish rose."

Stephen's response was to take her hand. "Perhaps you are right. But whatever the color of that rose, I'm hoping you and your pink cheeks will dine with me tonight."

April sighed as she watched the pink sky turn orange. It was such a pleasure to remember their first meeting. Later, when they used roses as a code, it made Stephen's spy work seem fun.

"Pink roses are fine."

"Because you are mine," April chimed in.

"But run fast as hell when I wear red," Stephen warned.

"Or we both may end up very dead."

"This is serious!" Stephen had grabbed her shoulders. "I don't want to lose you! You don't know how much I worry about you! Please! I don't care if it is a bush, bouquet, or boutonniere. Roses are the clue."

Once, they were meeting at a park. He was carrying pink roses, so she approached only to see him throw them to the ground and stomp on them. Instead of running to his side, she decided it must have originally been safe for them to meet but now meeting was dangerous. She walked back to her apartment taking several confusing detours in case she was being followed. Stephen met her there three hours later.

"You understood the clue..." April thought Stephen almost purred as he carried her to bed.

April had never felt love so tender...and then so passionate. She felt true happiness was finally hers — until the next morning when he gave her a present. It was a very small, very deadly, gun. "Please carry this always."

"Not to school!"

"I cannot always protect you, and people will eventually come."

"I'd never talk! Even if they tortured me!"

Stephen's eyes twinkled, and after a few jokes about "his mighty gun" more lovemaking had followed.

Suddenly, April realized that the sun had set. She had found no roses and she had not gone home. She looked around, saw nothing, and began walking down the path. Reaching the tree, she noticed the battery was gone. What was an old car battery doing on a walking trail anyway? April looked at her clothing. Her jacket was bright but the rest of her clothing was dark. Removing the gun and keys from her jacket and putting them in her shirt pocket, she nonchalantly dropped the jacket before running into the darkness.

She left the trail and took to the thicket. It was awkward, and sometimes painful, crawling through the brambles, but she maintained her silence by keeping her teeth clenched. Once she crawled through the end of the thicket, she quickly found her car, unlocked the door, and sped away.

Home was full of lovely smells. Stephen was busy cooking dinner and called out to her to "be ready to experience the virtues of the potato!" She was glad he wasn't upset by her lateness, but something felt wrong. Then, through the mist of roasting chicken and potato soup, she saw the message she'd received on the floor. He hadn't seen it.

Stephen's voice floated to her through the potato fog. "April, where did that car battery come from?"

Although her reaction was quick, she felt as if she were moving in slow motion. Pushing Stephen out the door, into the car, and driving down the street while she was trying to explain seemed almost as if she was watching someone else do it.

The explosion rocked the car despite their being two blocks away by the time it detonated.

April barely managed to get the car to the side of the road before Stephen pulled her into his arms. He pressed his lips on hers, but she pushed him away so that she could finish telling him about the battery. Tears of shame pierced her cheeks when she confessed that she hadn't left despite there being no rose, but she brushed the tears aside and managed to describe how she'd crawled through the thicket of thorns.

"They were hoping to catch us both on the trail," Stephen quietly said. "Which means one thing."

April looked up at him. She wanted him to know that she'd already guessed the truth. "They think I know something so now they want us both." Stephen nodded.

"When you came to the trail alone, they moved the bomb to the apartment."

"But Stephen, at least I did things right in the end."

April felt Stephen's strong arms around her again. His heartbeat pounded in rhythm with her own.

"Perhaps I don't need to worry about you so much," Stephen whispered, "I've been so in love with you that I've been blind – blind to how much you've learned! But please, let me worry just a little, if only for old time's sake. My April Rose. Who now takes care of me."

©2017 Leslie Muzingo

About the Author: Leslie Muzingo grew up in Iowa but relocated to the Deep South some years ago. She has recently began spending her summers in Prince Edward Island and finds great similarities between PEI and the rural Iowa of her youth. She was published in last year's Iowa State Writers Guild, The World Retold, (2016). Her stories have also been found in "Literary Mama", (2015) and Puff Puff Prose Poetry and a Play (2015). She considers herself an emerging writer. Her emergence is a slow one, as she has so many things she likes to do, and there are only so many hours in a day. She recently had a story published in the anthology, "Two Eyes Open" by MacKenzie Publishing. Another story of Leslie's will appear this spring in "The Forgotten and the Fantastical, IV" by Mother's Milk Books.

Follow Leslie on Twitter @sootfoot5.

"Tripping on a Blue Hole in a Paper Heart"

by Begoña Montesinos

Whispering, stunningly beautiful landscape wrapped around my heart as magic is revealed to me in a second. As a cure to my grieving soul, crawling while lost in a picturesque forest made of paper heart and loneliness. Could it be the perfect dream, everything we, as tiny beings, aspire to? Drizzle all over, bouncing, caressing heaven on ground, minimal consciousness embraced by the sweetest and fragile touch. Maybe God-like paradise creating a blue symphony of what is to be loved, or is it just me and my journey to the never ending pure land of fertile leaves and trees?

I was waiting for the brightest of the suns to wake me up when I saw her, carrying the mildest tenderness as a halo, that of the blessed born, the unique creatures who shine on us. She, goddess of our debilitating Earth, was to name me, or should I say, call me by using no words. Words, oh, they lost their meaning, breathless, abandoning me as an ethereal but fresh breeze dancing in the air, eyes closed.

Feeling a thick fog all around my invisible body, which played dead, numb by the night, whose dark curtain used to announce and welcome the yellow moon in me. Did she call my name? Was I tripping on a hole, embedded by the perfect fantasy? Who I was to meet?

Navigate, sail the infinite ocean ahead of me, timing the unexplored rhythm that creates the beating of my half heart. Lost in an immense and vast feeling of fulfillment when being surrounded by deepness and the mysterious hand of the unknown. Shaking the very human in me, I surrender and show my humbleness by landing on safe grounds. Terrified by the mundane that is to reside in us, feeling the earth moving under my feet, spiraling out of control in a turbulence, grabbing my hand tightly. Would I ever be the same person again? Not to be answered. Not in a near future. Not now.

What is to be known seems to vanish in a frivolous and forgettable moment out of logic in this world full of hatred. No remorse to be counted as guilt. Yet we flow together in a cloud, dense as the not revealed secret that lies upon us, that of the unselfish and pure love, that of giving and sharing regardless of conventions. What are they made of? Who is to blame? Get away from me!

And I arrived to that precious lake when opening my eyes. I was able to see her again above the bluest waters, transparent, drawing a colorful landscape for me and walking a clear path, that of heaven - of the peaceful warriors who decorate our history every single second in a temple of truth. This was made to be caressed, a sanctuary evolving patiently as an inner smile that grows constantly and effortlessly so as to make us happy. No material things anymore. No broken promises in disguise. Just pure emotions, our naked truth. Could it be magic? Say yes, please. Adhesive fire showering my painful tears in you. Breathing stronger, grasping for some air. Where are you now? Tell me, are you here?

Driving an empty road, frozen as I touch the blue sky, extremely cold, feeling the warmest embrace as an unexpected welcome. How can happiness be measured? The sun goes down as I pull over and feel the cool air in me. Trying to find my way through snowy terrains so as not to get lost. Is she there lighting my path now? Flawless, unrecognizable, me reaching you, waiting for the shining star at large, is it on the loose? Afraid of losing myself there. Ah, life in blue, dressed in joy and picturing harmony forever.

Blue, blue everywhere as if silent palettes of the sky artist were to be me, you, both dressed as one, covered in foggy clothes. Breaking apart, running, falling deep…Why us? Where is my heart to be? Frantic escape to the land, my secret garden again…Craving to caress the open seas that are to approach my soul. Come now. Waiting, impatiently, for her to be my silent witness. Come now…I whispered, incessantly, breathless, agonizing, begging for more air…

Begging for air, begging for life, craving more air. Where is her halo? Walking in unexplored paths and wondering if an end would draw more colors in me, in you, in us…Trying to find our way out of the mundane… and here comes the brightest of the suns, predicting an ethereal victory. Thus showing the real truth in us: craving. Pending feelings enrolled in a silent war within…within me and devouring the anger for more. Grasping for the vibrant emotion that is to reside in me, in you, in us.

Tripping on a blue hole where I hide my true self, where I can express my need for a vast land growing colorful landscapes in me, in us, in this truly impressive land ahead of us. And I reminisce of those ancient days full of joy: conquering, crawling inner smiles that are to diminish my growing pains…Breathing strongly, fresh new leaves in bloom, flying high in your smiling heart…come to me, I said…my Sanctuary in you…

And I see the Blue color surrounding every minute, every hour of my true existence beyond this silent world, getting brighter and creating a score of unique music to be released: You. Tempting, captivating, recreating emotions growing louder, incessantly louder; infinite emotions challenging the very silent wind in me, in you, in us…Approaching storm of unexplored feelings: Deep.

Tripping on a blue hole I grow bigger, my soul flying higher than birds, all over the mountains, as far as I wish, in ancient lands where pureness of love used to live once. Let's get together as one, a marvelous paper heart hidden in gold silent words whispering unity, forgotten empathy of the broken dreams, holding all the pieces together. Just feel it winning.

©2017 Begoña Montesinos

About the Author: I was born in Santa Cruz de Tenerife (Canary Islands, Spain), a beautiful city that embraces my soul every day. I live in ancient La Laguna (Unesco World Heritage Center) with my partner. I'm an English teacher who really enjoys what I do, that is, getting to inspire others and motivate them to be better and have a precious smile at all times. I do believe in love and following your heart no matter what. I see empathy as the most powerful weapon ever since it can change the world! I love to travel as traveling is my passion: it is what defines me as a person. Also I love to read and write. I take photographs as I walk this life through mysterious paths. I consider myself lucky enough to teach and learn during the process...education is a unique tool. Music is what makes my heart happy, my life, my everything. It is what creates a symphony within. I do believe in us, humans, and our ability to draw picturesque landscapes where others just see a deep void. The future is in us...Rise and love your peers as we aspire to be united and join as one!

Twitter:_@tricky_b47
Viewbug: tricky_b

"Better Off"

by Sarah Gilligan

Tonight was the big debate—the election was just a week away—so Karen got the kids to bed a little early while I washed up the dishes. She came back down, turned on the TV and changed the channel before flopping onto the couch.

"Want a beer?" I called from the kitchen, looking into the fridge.

"No, Coke's good."

I opened her can and my bottle, and brought in a bag of pretzels. While Carter and Reagan and the moderators were introduced, I got settled and put my feet up on the table. I nodded toward the screen as the first question was asked.

"Let the carnival begin."

I was just so sick of Carter and his weak ways, the high interest rates and all of it, even his dumb accent. It was obvious we needed a change—needed to be America again. I was hoping Reagan would just shut Jimmy down fast tonight, but they got going and after a while. My mind started wandering.

We'd been watching for almost an hour when I heard it.

"He asks his thirteen-year-old daughter for advice? Really?"

Karen nodded. "I get that he's a family man, but still."

"Amy Carter for President." I got up to take a leak and grabbed another beer on my way back.

"Nothing for me, thanks," Karen said in a flat tone.

"Oh, yeah, sorry." I sat down, ate the last pretzels and took a good, long drink. "What'd I miss?"

"Carter's calling Reagan dangerous and radical."

I snorted. "Better than a do-nothing wimp. Go back to the peanut farm, Jimmy."

"He means well. I just don't know if he has what it takes. But that Reagan, he's such an actor."

"Karen, of course he's an actor. They're all actors. But Carter, he's just a loser. Can't even get our hostages back. Who wants a loser running things? For Christ's sake, the whole country's been sitting around, licking its wounds and feeling bad about itself. So tired of it. Reagan's gonna make things happen."

"Reagan's telling us what we want to hear. People gobble that up."

"So you're saying it's all a scam?" I drank, picked at the label, then drank again. "I think I can tell if someone's bullshitting me."

"I didn't say that, Jeff," Karen said flatly. "You're the one who said they're all actors."

"Yeah. So you choose the movie you want to see. You want action or a boo-hoo weepie?"

Karen didn't answer and we went back to watching. During the closing statements, she started to nod off. Finally, she stretched and said she needed to get to bed.

After she went upstairs, I listened to the commentators talking about what Reagan had said: "Are you better off now than four years ago?" Sitting there on the couch, I thought about my life four years ago. Heather was barely two, Michael was a baby, and we weren't getting any sleep. Four years before that, Karen and I were newlyweds. We were crowded into my crappy old apartment, and I was just getting started selling insurance.

And twelve years ago? I was twenty in '68 and working drywall for my uncle. The war was getting crazy, but I had a deferral thanks to my penicillin allergy. How funny was that? They didn't want me to fight because I might die. Still, I felt like I could be dragged in at any time. Like they could change their minds and say, "You. Now." I remember all that year feeling like my life was hanging in the air, dangling, waiting for me to reach out and grab it before Uncle Sam took it away.

And of course, I thought about Rocco, my buddy Rocco. One day toward the end of that summer, we called in sick, went down to Misquamicut and met these two girls from Warwick on the beach. They had these broad Rhode Island accents — "Rawww-co!" — but they were really pretty, so we joked and flirted with them all morning, then grabbed some lunch and beers together. Back on the beach, I fell asleep on my towel to the sound of the girls gabbing and laughing. Next thing I knew, somebody shook my arm and I woke up all groggy and buzzed, the sun stinging my shoulders. I opened my eyes to see one of the girls, Michelle, sitting next to me. She had a head of soft black curls and her belly spilled a little over the top of her bikini, but not too much. She told me the others were in the water, then she leaned down and kissed me. The sun had been pounding on my face, so bright, until Michelle's head blocked the light and everything was suddenly cool. I tasted the sourness of beer and the sweetness of strawberry lip gloss. We sucked faces for a while, then got up and ran into the ocean together. Rocco and the other girl were heading back to the towels, so Michelle and I hung out past where the waves were breaking. Bobbing up and down, we kissed some more and slipped our hands inside each other's bathing suits. Twelve years later and I could still remember her hands and lips, the chill of the ocean, and the sharp heat of my body.

On the drive back from Rhode Island, I told Rocco about me and Michelle in the ocean. He didn't believe me, kept telling me I was full of shit. I showed him Michelle's phone number written down on a paper bag, but he grabbed it and started goofing around. As we flew up Route Two, he let it slip out the window. I socked his shoulder and yelled at him for a while, but he swore it was an accident, and by the time we hit the Hartford traffic, we were laughing about it. What the hell, it was like it had never even happened, like I had made up the whole thing.

A month later Rocco got called up for the draft and the next spring he was KIA on Hill 937, and that was that.

On the TV, the so-called experts were done talking, so I got up and shut it off, carried my empties and Karen's soda can to the kitchen and turned off the lights. Upstairs in the dark, Karen snored softly, and even though it took me a long time to get to sleep, I left her alone.

About the Author: For Sarah, it's all about the words. She is currently completing The Genius of Connecticut: her collection of linked short stories, and has previously written a series of essays about her tangle with breast cancer. She has helmed Cerebration, her writing and graphic design firm, for more than twenty-five years. She recently earned an honorable mention in the 2017 Short Story America Prize. Sarah lives in Connecticut with her husband and two daughters.

"Emerald Eyes"

by Leslie Muzingo

The last stretch of new train tracks had been laid in catty-corner fashion. Funny how the engineer who directed this strange design was never seen again once the last spike was driven and the champagne toast drunk. Perhaps he knew the chaos he'd caused and wanted to get away before his crime was discovered. Those passengers returning to the station had no problems as the tracks were split, and only the tracks for outgoing trains were affected. But what an affect those catty-cornered train tracks had on those who dared to ride! You'd think you were on the train to Boston and arrived in Timbuktu, or to New York and found yourself lost in Shanghai. It was unbelievable. It was magical.

"It's so much fun!" declared a pretty girl I met on the afternoon train from Baltimore to Istanbul. Scratch that. She wasn't pretty. Like the train ride, she was unbelievable. She was magical. She was oh so very fun! She was also the loveliest, most vibrant creature I'd ever seen, this girl with sparkling emerald eyes and hair like a western sunset. Was it because I was shy that her taking my hand emboldened me to speak? I stammered out my admiration for her beauty, and her laugh both charmed and comforted me like one of my best memories.

"You're a sly one," she said, her voice with an Irish lilt, and she gave my hand a squeeze as if applying balm to my troubled soul, adding, "I like that."

That's how my empty life suddenly became perfect. Each day Fiona and I tried a new destination, and each day was a sweet surprise. We bought tickets for Switzerland to see the staircase Traversinertobel bridge.

"We'll race across it!" Fiona said, clapping her hands with excitement. Reading the fear in my eyes, she promised, "If you catch me, you can kiss me." The train stopped in Bangkok, not Switzerland, so we rode an elephant instead of climbing the bridge. That night I dreamed of chasing her. In August, Fiona begged for cool weather. We bought tickets for Moscow.

"I don't speak Russian, do you?" she whispered from the corner of her mouth. "Not a word," I stage-whispered back.

"Russia is where the train will stop if the wee men have their way," she said with her eyebrows raised high. "Get your best spy face ready."

Maybe the train was listening. While we didn't end up in Russia, neither of us spoke a word of Eskimo either. At least Fiona no longer found the weather too hot, she even asked me to put my arms around her to protect her from the cold.

"Do you trust me?" I asked, my voice almost a gasp because of the lump in my throat. Fiona moved closer to me.

"Of course, Johnny."

Her trusting me simultaneously filled me with unbelievable joy, whilst also making me almost cry with pain. Sometimes, she'd bring a thermos of hearty Irish stew. Other days she'd pack a picnic basket of home baked foods. But, when we'd come upon just the right restaurant, only eating there would make our day complete.

Once, we planned a picnic in Yosemite and found ourselves in Tiananmen Square outside of the biggest dim sum house in the world. While Fiona's lunches were always lovely, we agreed dim sum like this might never come again. Besides, I liked buying Fiona lunch; her face glowed with childlike surprise when she tasted something new. She, in turn, liked sending me home with any uneaten picnic food. Lying in bed that night, I ate her sandwiches and pondered on how to make my home our permanent destination.

I was eating more than ever, so I was surprised when my brother Mark said I was losing weight. "You are skin and bones, John. What's up? It's been almost a year since—"

I stopped him. No point going there. I had traveling to do, and I had someone wonderful to travel with.

The next day felt special, like something was going to happen. I asked Fiona where she'd like to go, and she replied, "Wherever the train takes us."

She leaned her head on my shoulder. Once I heard her sigh. When I felt the train slow down, I cleared my throat and took her hand. She looked at me with those familiar emerald green eyes and smiled, but her eyes no longer sparkled and her smile was sad.

I kissed her. "Fiona, will you marry me?"

"Johnny, you know I'm not the lass for you."

The fog raced in—curling, menacing, smoking fog—and my heart stopped. Then the conductor called out, "Kinsale, County Cork! Everyone off for Kinsale, County Cork!"

They tell me that I screamed for a long time and that it wasn't till the doctor injected me with something that I stopped. I think there were a lot of injections, but I'm not sure. I don't remember much before the shock treatments.

I let the doctor believe that I've now accepted that Caitlin dying wasn't my fault. But it was. We'd both been drinking. She insisted on driving us back to her parent's house because she knew the way better in the fog than I did. When the car stalled on the tracks, I jumped out and thought she would too. She sat there mesmerized, her emerald eyes staring into the lights of the oncoming train. I screamed – I ran to save her – I was too late.

Do Irish deer have green eyes?

I killed Caitlin and I killed Fiona. If I'd driven that night, Caitlin would be alive. If I'd fought against the shock treatments, I'd be traveling with Fiona. The doctor claimed Fiona wasn't real, and my brother brought my passport with no new stamps in it since the trip to Ireland I made with Caitlin, as proof that Fiona did not exist.

I do not believe the disbelievers.

I went to the train station immediately upon discharge from the hospital. In fact, I can't seem to stay away. I know my vigil there is to punish myself for not saying yes yes yes Fiona, I will chase you across the bridge. Maybe I need to watch the destruction of my dream; I need to allow the wee men to show me what might have been. Either way, the difference between what I must live now and what I had then is clear.

Rail by rail and spike by spike, the catty-cornered section of track is being ripped out and replaced with a forward moving track. Onlookers nod approvingly. How quickly people are willing to give up on magic—but I will not give up on love!

About the Author: Leslie Muzingo grew up in Iowa but relocated to the Deep South some years ago. She has recently begun spending her summers in Prince Edward Island and finds great similarities between PEI and the rural Iowa of her youth. She was published in last year's Iowa State Writers Guild, The World Retold, (2016). Her stories have also been found in "Literary Mama", (2015) and Puff Puff Prose Poetry and a Play (2015). She considers herself an emerging writer. Her emergence is a slow one as she has so many things she likes to do, and there are only so many hours in a day. She recently had a story published in the anthology, "Two Eyes Open" by MacKenzie Publishing. Another story of Leslie's will appear this spring in "The Forgotten and the Fantastical, IV" by Mother's Milk Books.

Follow Leslie on Twitter @sootfoot5.

"The Fastest Rockslinger in the West"

by Leslie Muzingo

It was the land of big sky. It was a harsh land without trees for summer shade or protection from winter's blizzard winds. The white man dared not forget that the Sioux was King. David understood this rule of royalty and even agreed with it. Nebraska was his heart's home.

His father left for California with others who dreamed of gold. He sent a letter by way of a stranger traveling east. He'd made it to a Jesuit Mission in San Luis Obispo. The priests were kind and promised to direct him to a place to mine for gold. He'd write when he could.

Two years passed without another letter.

David decided to find his father. He packed his kit and kissed his weeping mother. His kiss awoke something within her. Her eyes flashed.

"Stay! If your father didn't come back, neither will a young man like you!"

"You know how good a shot I am?" His mother nodded. David pulled a sling out of his coat pocket. 'did you know that I'm even better with this sling than I am with a gun?" A melancholy smile filled his mother's face. David continued,

"I was a child when you gave me this sling. I remember you saying, "Guns run out of bullets, but you can always find rocks." Mother, because of you I can do this!" He mounted his horse and left.

David quickly understood how the Badlands got its name. It wasn't merely because there was no water, it was because the wind blew with such evil intent that it seemed to sing Satan's song. David was glad to move on into Utah Territory where the breezes crooned a cheerful tune so melodious that it almost saddened him to turn south into California.

He came upon some miners resting around a fire. One was picking a lonesome refrain on an old guitar. They welcomed David until he asked about San Luis Obispo. As if in one voice, they let forth a cynical laugh.

"What's so funny?" David asked, his eyes narrowed.

The oldest miner sighed. "Nothing. We laugh so we do not cry. You will not find whomever you seek in San Luis Obispo."

"Explain!"

The miners all spoke at once.

—The bandits make the priests trick these men!

—They could stop if they tried!

—Priests cannot fight bandits!

—What they do is a great sin!

—They will rot in hell!

David left. He had heard enough. David pressed southward until he found the Jesuit mission. He stayed out of sight and waited.

His wait was short. The next day he saw a band of Mexicans ride toward the mission. Their horses' saddles were decorated with silver. The Mexicans wore large hats unlike any David had seen, and their ammunition was strapped across their backs.

The priests introduced several white men. One bandit's laughter echoed through the air. "Si! We take you to mine for gold!" The white men mounted their horses and joined the Mexicans. David briefly waited before he tracked them across the dusty landscape.

At twilight, the bandits stopped at an adobe hut. The white men were taken away by one of the bandits while the others went into the hut. Soon David heard singing, and he smiled remembering the men in the saloon back home.

In a few hours the Mexicans, who had ridden all day in the hot sun, were drunk off their tequila and asleep. David inched his way to the bandit's horses. He gently took their reigns, led them far away, and tied them securely so neither the horses nor the bandits could bolt when the shooting started.

The only company David had that night was from one lone rattlesnake. He'd stuffed the snake in a leather sack thinking it might make good eating later.

By morning, David was ready for the gunfight to begin. He smiled when he heard the cries of, "Jefe nuestros caballos se han ido!" All this meant to David was that it was time to aim his rifle at the door.

Men, still in their underwear, poured out into daylight. David fired and two men went down. He picked up his other rifle and aimed for the fully dressed man running as fast as his short, fat legs could go. One shot, and the man ran no more.

David waited. He watched a tumbleweed bounce pass him and, out of the corner of his eye, he saw a bandit trying to escape from the back of the hut. He let the man make his dash, then David let go with the other barrel of his rifle. David watched the man twitch in pain as he reloaded. Death ended the bandit's twitching by the time David's rifles were full of bullets once more.

By David's count the only bandit remaining was the main boss, the one who'd laughed so loudly while at the mission. David waited several hours, but the door did not open a crack.

The sun rose high in the sky. David figured it must be hot in that hut now and that the bandit was probably sitting right under what served for a window. With extreme care, David loaded the rattlesnake into the sling. He swung the sling high over his head and aimed for the opening. The snake flew in a high arch and landed with a heavy thud inside the hut. The bandit screamed like a girl and ran out the door, across the dry dirt, and stood not fifty feet from where David sat on his horse.

The man must've planned on waiting until dark to escape because he was still in his underwear and had no gun or boots. He fell to his knees.

"WHO ARE YOU?" he screamed. His cry, like his laugh, echoed.

"A boy who seeks vengeance for his father," David said. "Now run."

"What?"

David twirled the sling over his head.

"RUN!"

The bandit zig-zagged across the dry terrain. Whether his movements were an attempt to dodge the rock or he was frightened of the spiders and scorpions that ran across the cracked earth, David neither knew nor cared. As always, David's aim was true. The rock, after flying in a perfect arch, hit the bandit in the head so hard that it was as if he'd been shot with a bullet. He was killed instantly.

David found his father and twenty-two other men chained together and mining for gold. The bandits always took all the gold they found, but one man knew where it was stashed. They loaded the gold on the horses, and together they walked to the nearest village.

David and his father were glad to head back to Nebraska, the land of the Big Sky.

David couldn't get word to his mother, but she learned of her son's victory. Someone had shown her a San Francisco newspaper. Blazed across the front page, it said: "Fastest Rock-slinger Thwarts Corrupt Priests, Kills Bandits, Saves Dad!" She prayed a thank-you to heaven and asked God to save her from pride. Then, the woman in her began making a list on how she'd spend her husband's gold.

©2017 Leslie Muzingo

About the Author: Leslie Muzingo grew up in Iowa but re-located to the Deep South some years ago. She has recently begun spending her summers in Prince Edward Island and finds great similarities between PEI and the rural Iowa of her youth. She was published in last year's Iowa State Writers Guild, The World Retold, (2016). Her stories have also been found in "Literary Mama", (2015) and Puff Puff Prose Poetry and a Play (2015). She considers herself an emerging writer. Her emergence is a slow one as she has so many things she likes to do, and there are only so many hours in a day. She recently had a story published in the anthology, "Two Eyes Open" by MacKenzie Publishing. Another story of Leslie's will appear this spring in "The Forgotten and the Fantastical, IV" by Mother's Milk Books.

Follow Leslie on Twitter @sootfoot5.

"Sticker Shock"

by Leah Holbrook Sackett

On the first day in August, I wasn't looking for a table. I wasn't looking for anything. I was just window shopping at the resale shop while I waited for my friend, Lena, to show up for Sunday brunch. It was her birthday, and she was turning 42. This was our girls' day out to celebrate. I was early, and she would be late, as usual. I kept watch out the window for her arrival. Then, I saw the antique Chippendale style table done in the 18th century mode. Oh my God, it was gorgeous, with cabriole legs executed in the Philadelphia Rococo School of Design, which were carved with the Acanthus leaf motif, coupled with the carved volutes and ruffles ending in the claw-and-ball feet. Plus, it had a heavy and deep, reflective Mahogany table top set round with 8 chairs. It was outside my price range as well. The price tag read $11,787, including the chairs. The beautiful trapezoidal seats were upholstered in a buttery, soft yellow cotton twill, with the cabriole legs and carved Acanthus leaf motif ending in the elegantly carved claw-and-ball feet, a perfect match with the table. Oh, it was lovely. In comparison, it felt so graceful, exotic and unlike anything I owned. My furniture was all straight, clean lines. I took a turn around the store to mull things over while looking at tarnished silverware, hurricane lamps, a section of old jazz on vinyl, a four-poster cherry wood bed with a chunk of wood missing from the bottom of one leg, old mink coats, a collection of Underwood typewriters. In this ruminative manner, I forgot about Lena. Once I remembered, I texted her that I was in Ye Old Shoppe across the street from the restaurant, "Breakfast at Tiffany's."

With that taken care of, I circled back to the table. I did not need a dining room table, per se. But I did not have one, either. Not that it even remotely matched any of my modern furniture in the house. But the dining room was empty. It even echoed. We ate all our meals in the living room, on the sofa, while watching TV. We were binge watchers, too. Right now, we were working on Better Call Saul. I mean, how often was I really going to use a dining room table. Michael and I were not going to give up our dinners with Saul Goodman. In fact, I didn't even use the small kitchen table I did have, not properly. That small drop-leaf table in the kitchen wasn't used for anything except to collect mail, umbrellas, my purse, and whatever else was in my hands on my way into the house. So really, I did not need this beautiful table that didn't match, but I wanted it. I really wanted it. Perhaps we could host Thanksgiving this year with a table like that. See what this table was doing to me, already roping me into hosting family dinners with both sides, oh, the nightmare. Was I crazy to be contemplating this at all? And there still wouldn't be enough chairs for everyone. I'd still have to set up card tables and folding chairs. How would I decide who was seated at the Chippendale table and who was seated at the card table? I could not even begin to address the family politics of such a situation. Still I wanted this table. I began thinking of the table runners, table cloths (although it would be a shame to ever cover that beautiful mahogany), vases, and flowers with which I could dress the table for the different seasons. Then, I felt someone hovering close to me. I thought it was Lena, but it was a woman in a green cloche hat. And it looked good on her. Hats never looked good on me. She was eyeing the table. She even stooped down to examine the graceful legs. It felt like such a violation. It was as if I could feel her hand running up and down my own leg. When she stood up, she placed her fingertips on the tabletop and pressed down firmly, claiming a tentative grasp on my table. I panicked. I yelled out to the store keeper,

"I'll take this table."

"It's only part of a set," she said. "It comes with the sideboard and the hutch."

"That's wonderful," I blurted.

I had just committed to a table with 8 chairs, a sideboard, and a hutch. Each with their own price tag.

Well, hell, what was the package price going to be? I wondered. When the woman in the green cloche hat moved away I saw a su-persized price tag that I had failed to notice before hanging from the hutch. It read Chippendale set $17,483.

Shit.

My heart was pounding in my throat. How was I going to ex-plain this to Michael? It was not like me to make impulsive pur-chases; that was more his thing. Crap. In fact, I was constantly dog-ging him about being mindful of spending. The sales woman came over and asked if that would be cash, check, or charge. I dug into my purse and reluctantly handed her my charge card. Just then, I heard the tinkle of the bell over the front door, and I looked up to watch the women in the green cloche hat make her exit, that bitch. Just then, Lena entered. Fantastic, all I had got her was a dainty, whimsical necklace that cost me $30 and now she was about to witness me spending $17,483 on myself. I felt like a fool and a heel. I felt like crying.

But Lena was super supportive about the table, and then about the rest of the sea of furniture I floundered in the midst of like a survivor of a sinking ship. With my receipt in hand, all I could think was how was I going to get this antique furniture home? I didn't even have a friend with a truck.

About the Author: Leah Holbrook Sackett is an adjunct lecturer in the English department at the University of Missouri - St. Louis. This is also where she earned her M.F.A. Additionally, she has published short stories in several journals such as Connotation Press, Blacktop Passages, Crack the Spine, and Halfway Down the Stairs. Finally, Leah lives with her husband Jonathan and daughter Bella in Webster Groves, and she is a curious member of the Lewis Carroll Society of North America. You can learn more about Leah's writing at www.leahholbrooksackett.com.

"Blue Crush"

by Sheila Rosart

The acid spew is worse this time. As the blistering geyser shoots into the blood-orange colored sky, I despair of ever being happy again. Another re-lo, another colony, another quadrant. What's the point? I can't even conceive of a post-apocalyptic pop song that would cheer me up.

There are fifteen other humans in my tube and about six un-assigned; maybe part-human, mostly synthetic, wrapped in digitized e-skin. The one nearest me is an interesting shade of blue and illuminates our tube with a pretty phosphorescence that stabs through the usual blackness. I move closer, eager to keep my ocular perceptions acclimated so I'm not blinded by landing-light when we arrive.

As we blast below the pocked surface of Evergreen, I contemplate my new reality. More strangers, more physical evolution, and a pseudo-environment probably more shockingly inhospitable. Though, it would be hard to beat the toxic spew of H-I95-C.

"Breathing protocol initiated," says the voice in my ear receptors. Along with the others, I switch out the oxygenated tube on the right for the fluting on the left and activate my prosthetic lung. Thank CEO mine inflates; you just never know.

Coughing and choking as my body adjusts to breathing radiation vapor, I manage to knock loose my new earring; a pearly cluster of moonstones that cost me a month's worth of chits. I feel it slide down my protected mobility unit and lodge near my navel. Shit!

"Level II, Mach IV speed. Initiating stupor setting," drones the holo attendant in a gender-fluid, and obnoxiously cheery synthetic voice.

I regain awareness at three moons Evergreen time, but since I don't know what time we left, I'm clueless as to how long I've been out.

We'd lost three humans if the sagging suits were anything to go by, and one of the un-defined looks like he's in full rigor. I suspect he got over-vapored or had a faulty suit. I'm glad my little blue friend is still glowing healthily at my side; it means I'm not blind.

Turning my head into the plush lining of my helmet, I manage to wipe the drool from my lips. I feel my earring summersault into the nether regions of my VMU and then cartwheel down my left leg into the base of my suit. Damn it! Now I would probably crush it when I had to walk.

That'll teach me to spend e-coin on ancient symbols of beauty. But I do love a glittery bauble. Probably some vain, atavistic hold-over from when people had to attract partners, instead of swiping-right on chemical e-match sites. Either that or I have magpie blood.

Blue guy sidles in close to me and initiates a message. I switch on Accept and Translate.

"You alright? No distress?" is what he sends. That was sweet, so I reply.

"Actually, lost an earring down my suit; it was new. Stupid."

"Sorry. Can I help?"

Ok, that was creepy. "Unlikely, but thanks," I send back.

"Does it have a metallic nature?"

What is it with this guy? He's obsessed with my fucking jewelry. That makes two of us, but at least my concern is justified.

"Titanium-core alloy, moonstones."

"I can retrieve it for you."

Yeah, sure. I bet he wants me to de-suit so he can retrieve my organic body parts! I know how valuable a fresh harvest is on the market. That's where I got my new right arm after the bacterial leach on Surnia dissolved my old one. And it wasn't cheap. We're talking five million turbo chits. Plus tax.

"That's ok. Not de-suiting till arrival, but thanks."

"I'm magnetized."

"Repeat." Just my luck, I get packed next to a narcissistic, talkative perv during evac.

"I have a magnetic prosthesis. No need to de-suit."

Well, that puts a different spin on things.

"Ok, go for it," I say, closing my eyes and bracing for the burn.

There's a little tingle near my left metatarsal and I feel the earring dislodge and begin to rise. I open my eyes, surprised it doesn't hurt.

What starts as a tingle slowly manifests into a gentle caress. Blue man is crouched at my ankles, pointing his gloved magnet at my leg and staring up at me with almond-shaped eyes, so green they have to be lensed. But they sure look great with his blue complexion.

It may be my distorted vision field, but I think he's grinning at me and there's something intimate about the way his gaze bores into mine.

As he rises, so does my earring and I can feel his finger gently pressing through my suit layers.

I look away to break his spell. Damn if he isn't initiating a sexual response. I try desperately to distract myself with thoughts of sun shear and icicle storms, but I can't seem to resist meeting his stare head on, like I'm anode to his cathode.

Travelling up the inside of my leg with his finger, painfully slowly, the pleasure sensation creeps towards my navel. I swear he pauses at the junction of my legs, but I can't be sure because now I'm shaky and worry I might tip over.

"Steady, there." His voice whispers in my ear. His voice, real or not, is a delicious blend of smooth baritone and Marlboro Man rumble. Auditory communication seems more appropriate to the occasion so I switch off message mode and let his voice wash over me.

"What's your name, beautiful?"

Practically incapable of speech, I force myself to croak out my name.

"Samira."

"I like it. I'm Maxwell, Samira. Whoa, are you doing ok?" he asks again as my legs crumple.

CEO knows what I reply, but this man is intuitive. Just then his other arm shoots around my waist and he backs me up against the side of our shuttle, preventing an embarrassing fall and possibly a fatal suit-breach.

"Shall I stop, Samira? You can always get the earring once you're domiciled again."

Lord no! He cannot possible stop now. "I'm ok. We've gone this far, might as well continue."

Who's the perv now?

We are eye-to-eye as the earring approaches my upper rib cage. The magnetic stimulation shoots little pulses through my nerve endings and I feel my every synapse on fire, worse than a volcanic scorch. But much more pleasant.

Now Max looks serious, strangely intense, and I wonder if this turns him on too. Just how much sensation can be imbued in prosthetics these days, anyhow? If only I'd paid attention in Bio Physics 102, I wouldn't be this physiologically ignorant.

Moonstones slither across my upper abdomen and towards my breasts. I can't believe we are in an evac tube headed for a safe haven after narrowly escaping death by petrochemical spout.

I find myself looking forward to the next re-lo.

Max the blue guy's helmet is touching mine and his eyes are closed. I follow suit so I can revel in pure tactile bliss. The earring glides over my breast, slipping past my shoulder and trailing up my neck.

My reverie is rudely interrupted by the arrival announcement.

"Oxygenated atmosphere detected. Commence disembarkation."

The doors are released just as the errant clump of moonstone lands on the lobe of my ear, welcomed back by the crisp click of its auto-clasp.

©2017 Sheila Rosart

About the Author: Sheila Rosart aspires to be tall, successful and well-moisturized, but has failed overwhelmingly in each regard. In her next life, she fully intends to be an award-winning writer, a toast-worthy literary sensation, or someone with really good hair. Usually found in San Antonio, TX, there is no telling what she does all day, but ignoring her children, husband and psychopathic pets is a full-time job.

"What Makes Us Human"

by Victoria Sylvander

"Ramona! Hey!"

"Oh, hi, Yuki. Did geometry get out on time for once?"

"Yeah. I might actually make the bus today."

"Hmm."

"Hey, are you okay? You look like you're about to be sick."

"I'm going to tell my parents today."

"What? Why?"

"Mom and Dad will be home at the same time for once. I could do it this weekend, but I'm sick of waiting."

"Oh, no. This again? I'm telling you, you've only got this idea because you've never dated anyone."

"Will you admit when you're wrong when I show up to our 10th reunion and don't bring a plus one?"

"Maybe our 20th reunion."

"Oh, thanks, that really helps."

"We're only 16. Date someone cute and give it time."

"Yeah. Sure. You'd better go; you're about to miss your bus."

❖ ❖ ❖

"Mom? Dad? I have to tell you something."

"What's wrong, honey? Did you and Yuki have a fight?"

"No, it…well…I'll just spit it out. I wanted to tell you that I'm asexual."

"Oh, honey…that can't be true."

"What the hell does that even mean, asexual? You have a sex; you're a girl."

"It means that I don't experience sexual attraction, not that I'm agender. Here, I printed these off of an asexuality website. They might help you understand."

"You teenagers. If you see it on the damn internet, you'll believe anything."

"Dad, hundreds of people identify as asexual. Please, just read these."

"If these people want to call themselves asexual, that's fine, but I'm sure they all have issues. There are illnesses that lower sex drive. You're young and healthy."

"Even if I did have some kind of disease, I would still be asexual."

"Nobody is really asexual, honey. Sex is what makes us human."

"Mom…are you serious? Animals have sex! Human as opposed to what, robots?"

"Don't take that tone with your mother, young lady!"

"But she's wrong!"

"I don't know if you really believe this shit or if you're just pulling this for attention, but either way, we're getting you a therapist."

"Good! Maybe you'll believe me with an expert backing me up!"

"You're not asexual, Ramona. No one is."

"Yes, I fucking am!"

"Language! That's it. Go to your room."

"Fine! I'll go on my favorite website and talk to some people who actually support me!"

"Terry…did you ever think we'd be having this conversation with our little girl?"

"No…God help us."

"It looks like we have a new member of the Pineview High Queer Alliance! I'm Jay Danvers. Would you mind introducing yourself?"

"Yeah, okay. Hi. I'm Ramona Tassler. I'm a junior. I play field hockey and ice hockey. I'm here because I need support, I guess. My family was pretty crappy when I came out."

"Well, we can give you plenty of support here."

"Thanks, that…that would be nice. My parents even said they would put me in therapy."

"Oh, shit. Conversion therapy?"

"I'm not sure. I hope it's real therapy, because I've been having some pretty dark thoughts about…about being queer, and how sick and wrong I feel. And I don't know if there's conversion therapy for being ace."

"Wait, being what?"

"Ace. Asexual."

"Oh…so are you same-gender attracted or trans?"

"Um…I don't know. I think I might be aromantic."

"Oh. Well, I'm going to have to ask you to leave."

"What? Why?"

"You have to be same-gender attracted or trans to be queer. This group is for queer people. We can't have you taking up resources."

"You're saying that even though I'm not straight, I'm not queer enough?"

"You're valid, but you're not queer. Please leave."

"Wow, really? Some support you assholes provide!"

"Come on, Jay, that was a little harsh. She might be a lesbian. Alison Bechdel thought she was asexual before she figured out she was gay."

"Okay, Lakeisha, you have a point. If that's true, she can come back. But right now, we don't need straight invaders."

"Hi, Ms. Channing. Thanks for seeing me on such short notice."

"It's no problem. I had a cancellation. Now, usually I start with a little getting-to-know-you…"

"Can we do that later? I've been feeling suicidal. I need to talk about it."

"Of course; it sounds like we need to talk about that. Do you feel like you're in danger?"

"Well, no. But I feel awful. Worthless. Like I'm not really human. Even the Queer Alliance kicked me out."

"I'm so sorry you're going through that. Why did the Queer Alliance's unfair rejection of you make you feel like you weren't really human?"

"Well, I'm asexual. That isn't queer enough, I guess. It made me feel like I don't fit in anywhere. And my mom said asexuality didn't exist. She and my dad are making me see a therapist. I mean, I guess therapy is okay, since I've been feeling so…so warped."

"I'm glad to hear you're open to the idea of therapy outside of school counseling. How do you think you would react to being diagnosed with female sexual interest disorder?"

"What?"

"Asexuality as a sexual orientation doesn't exist. Asexual-identified people have what used to be called hyposexual desire disorder. Now the name—at least for women—is female sexual interest disorder. Hormone therapy might be able to help you."

"My identity is not a fucking disorder!"

"Ramona, there's no need to be so hostile. If you are willing to listen..."

"I'm not if you're not!"

"Ramona...wait, come back!"

"Fuck the world, Yuki. Just...fuck the world."

"Why don't you tell me how you really feel?"

"I mean it! My parents, the Queer Alliance, even the fucking student counselor...they all suck. And my parents told me they found me a sex therapist who can turn me into a horn-ball."

"Eww."

"I know, right?"

"Ramona...don't you think you should at least give therapy a shot?"

"Are...are you serious?"

"Don't you think it's possible you're just a late bloomer?"

"Even if I am, there's nothing wrong with me! What the hell, Yuki? You're against me too?"

"I'm not against you! I just want you to be happy. I'm trying to help."

"That's not help, that's invalidation. And you can shove it up your ass."

"Whoa. Okay. Fuck you too, I guess."

"Tassler! I heard you really think you don't like dick or pussy! Want some of this dick? I can fix you!"

"You just need to be with a good lover. Like Emilie Autumn; she thought she was asexual until she got with someone who knew what they were doing."

"Asexuality doesn't exist. You're just trying to be a special snowflake."

"So do you not have, you know, junk?"

"I hope you get raped."

"Selfish bitch!"

"Frigid!"

"Freak!"

"Ramona. Ramona! We told you that therapy was this morning. Now get up."

"Ramona, honey, we know you don't want to go, but it's for your own good."

"Pretending to sleep isn't going to do you any…wait…oh…oh my God…"

"Ramona, trying to scare us like this isn't funny! Wake up!"

"Lisa, she's not trying to scare us! That's real blood!"

"Oh, God! Oh, God, no!"

"Ramona…Ramona, please wake up…!"

"Ramona! No, God, not my baby!"

"I'll call an ambulance!"

"No…*no*…"

"911? My daughter slit her wrists!"

"Terry, it's too late…she's gone."

About the Author: Victoria Sylvander is a queer disabled writer and loudmouth activist who started writing as soon as she could hold a pencil and never stopped. When she isn't writing (which is rare), she can be found absorbed in a book, playing World of Warcraft, snuggling with her cat, or rehearsing with her rock band. She received the email informing her that her story about acemisia had won the "It's All Dialogue" Short Story Contest for September 2017 on the first day of Asexuality Week. She was both amused by the timing and overjoyed. She hopes those who read her story can learn from it.

Keep up with Victoria on twitter at @sylvanasvictory and Instagram @highfemmewriter.

"Paper Mache Man"

by Steve Carr

Steam from the train pulling into the station blew in through the open window, filling Malcolm's third floor art studio with a hot, damp cloud.

"Damn," he muttered, quickly rushing to the window and pushing down the top frame.

He leaned his forehead on the pane of glass of the upper frame and watched the wheels come to a screeching stop at the platform. Moments later, the metal stairs were extended out from the doors and throngs of people began to rush out.

He turned away from the window and looked around the studio.

"Let's take care of your ear," he said to his dog, Scout, who was sitting on a rug under the large oak work table. Scout stood on his short, stout legs and wagged his stubby tail. Malcolm reached under the table and took the small dog in his arms and placed him on the table next to where Jarvis was stretched out. The dog sat on his rump, loudly panting.

Malcolm put a cup of flour in a bowl and then poured a cup of water and a half tablespoon of salt and stirred the mixture until it was a pasty consistency. He took a strip of newspaper and dipped it in the paste, then pulled it out and wiped off the excess paste, then put the strip on Scout's ear where a previously applied strip had ripped.

Rubbing the dog's back, Malcolm said to it, "There ya go boy, just like new."

Scout licked Malcolm's hand with its dry, stiff tongue. Malcolm set him back on the floor and turned to Jarvis.

"You've been very patient, Jarvis," he said. "I'll do your left knee-cap then we"re done."

Jarvis raised up on his elbows and looked down the length of his paper-mache body. Malcolm put several strips of newspaper in the paste mixture, then pulled them out and removed the excess paste, then put the strips on Jarvis' knee.

"You'll have to lay there until it's dried," Malcolm said. Jarvis laid back down.

Sitting at the counter in the train station diner, Malcolm stabbed at his Salisbury steak with his fork. Gracie, the waitress standing on the other side of the counter, gazed at him appraisingly.

"You're such a nice guy. Why are you always alone?"

"It's not easy making friends," he said. He put the money for the food along with a tip for Connie by his plate and pushed his way through the crowd until he made it to the magazine stand.

"What you got for me today, Harry?" Malcolm said to the leg-less man in a wheelchair behind the counter.

"Hey, Malcolm," Harry said. "I've got a bundle of old newspa-pers." Harry placed the newspapers that were tied together with twine onto the counter.

"What do I owe you, Harry?" Malcolm said.

"Five bucks should do it," Harry said. "I haven't asked before, but I'm curious. What do you do with all the old newspapers and magazines?"

Malcolm took a five-dollar bill out of his wallet. "I make things," he said.

Malcolm carried the armload of newspapers up the three flights of metal stairs and opened the door to his studio and saw Jarvis standing at the window, looking out.

"Jarvis, you should have let me make sure your knee was ready for you to stand on before getting off the table," Malcolm said as he pushed the door closed with his butt. Jarvis turned around.

Malcolm dropped the newspapers on the floor. Scout came out from beneath the table and rubbed his body against Malcolm's leg. Looking down at him, Malcolm said,

"Your ear looks much better, boy," and reached down and patted the dog's head. At the table, Malcolm said, "Come sit down, Jarvis. It's time to give you a face and some skin." Jarvis rambled over to the table and sat down.

Malcolm began arranging the paints and brushes on the table next to Jarvis. Three hours later, Jarvis was covered in flesh colored paint. He had a pair of dark green eyes and a full pink set of lips. The painted on hair on the top of his head was dark brown, as were his eyebrows and eyelashes. Inside his opened mouth, his teeth were painted pearl white and his tongue and the rest of the interior of his mouth was painted a dark pink. When finished, Malcolm stood back and said,

"Jarvis, you're a very handsome man. Go look at yourself in the mirror."

Jarvis hopped from the table and stepped over the cardboard boxes filled with clay pottery, baskets of yarn, bags of quilting squares and a stack of old crafts magazines to get to the floor length mirror. He stared at his reflection for several minutes before turning around and pointed at his mouth with his finger.

"I'll teach you how to talk later," Malcolm said. "Let's get you dressed in the new clothes I bought for you and I'll take you out to see the world."

Walking to the train station, Malcolm pointed out everything he could to Jarvis and said what it was and what it was used for. By the time they reached the station, Jarvis knew what a fire hydrant, telephone pole, manhole cover, mailbox, car, neon sign, trash can, bus stop and revolving door were.

Entering the station, Jarvis' fascination with people required Malcolm to pull him through the crowd to keep him from stopping and staring. At the diner counter he showed Jarvis how to sit on the stool, then sat down by him.

"I've made a friend," Malcolm said when Connie came over.

"Good for you," she said. "You're a real cutie," Connie said to Jarvis.

Jarvis stared at her, taking in every detail of Connie's appearance. "Water comes from the fire hydrant to put out fires," he said.

"He's practicing his English," Malcolm said.

"Where's he from?" Connie said.

"A bit of everywhere," Malcolm said. "I wanted him to meet you and see the train station. It's the best place to see how people come and go."

"I guess it is at that," Connie said. "What would you like to eat?"

"Nothing today, Connie," Malcolm said. "That will come later."

Taking Jarvis by the arm, Malcolm pulled him from the bench and back into the crowd. While exiting through the station doors, Malcolm fell on the ground. His leg was stepped on by a heavyset man whose arms were loaded with suitcases.

In the studio, Scout's tail wagged as he jumped up on Malcolm's leg. Malcolm picked the dog up and let it lick his face with his paper-mache tongue then put him down.

"My leg is injured," he said.

Jarvis sat on the stool in front of the loom. "Trash cans are picked up once a week," he said.

Malcolm tore some strips of newspaper and prepared a bowl of paste. He raised his pants leg and with his fingertips prodded the tear in his paper-mache skin on his lower leg.

He put the strip of paper on his leg.

About the Author: Steve Carr, who lives in Richmond, Va., began his writing career as a military journalist and has had over 160 short stories published internationally in print and online magazines, literary journals and anthologies. Sand, a collection of his short stories, was published recently by Clarendon House Books. His plays have been produced in several states in the U.S. He was a 2017 Pushcart Prize nominee. He is on Facebook https://www.facebook.com/profile.php?id=100012966314127 and Twitter @carrsteven960.

"Gloria's Verdict"

by Kate Huffman

It screams at her. Her body. Constantly screams. Pills help, but she knows those will kill her eventually. Doesn't always stop her.

He's snoring. Why shouldn't he be? She buries any urge to wake him and tries to breathe through a "pain release meditation."

It's garbage. Getting up means sharp electricity through every nerve ending, but she does it. Worse than the pain is her mood. Her spirits plummet because it's her fault and her fault alone, this pain. And she knows she's going to the gym today, despite this pain. She's an addict. She can't not.

In the living room now, she grabs a book off a shelf without looking to see what it is. She asks a question: Will I die this year?

She opens the book and points her finger at random. "At least we know who it is, can see who you are now, Gloria." She reads the sentence over and over, determined to make sense of it. Does this mean they will see who I am after I'm dead? They'll know who I am? So that's a yes?

She loves this game, bibliomancy. It's supposed to be played with a Bible, but she plays it with classics. She checks the book: Losing Battles by Eudora Welty. She always gets good answers from this one. She even calls the book "Gloria," because the character, Gloria, features so heavily in its answer.

Will it be within the next six months? She flips the pages and shoves in her finger for the answer, but then, he's there, standing in the doorway. His shoulders droop.

"Hey…"

"I'm fine, please go back to sleep." She doesn't move her finger. She's dying to know Gloria's answer but doesn't want to look rude.

His shoulders somehow manage to sink even further down. 'do you want me to sleep out here? Do you want the bed to yourself?"

"No, you're fine, please."

His chest bounces with shallow breathing. She stands, but not before sneaking a peak at the sentence:

"Still out floating on a boat, still the same scoundrel."

Ugh. That's a definite no. She'll be floating through life, scoundrel-ling away. Gloria just didn't point out that her boat is severely damaged and all scoundrelish behavior is against herself and herself alone.

She slams the book shut. "Don't be upset, I'll be fine."

But he saw her wince when she stood. It's bad tonight. And he knows it. When he squeezes the bridge of his nose, he's about to say something heartfelt. As if he's mustering the courage to be emotionally vulnerable.

She stops him before he has a chance by pulling his hand from his face and leading him back to bed. He's new enough in her life not to be bored by her chronic pain. In time, he'll get used to it, then gradually sick of it. Then he'll go. He'll hate himself, but he'll go. And she won't blame him. It's no fun to be around someone constantly in pain.

As she walks him back to the bedroom, she feels her thighs jiggle. Her hips scream—scream—with each step, but she feels her thighs jiggle and she knows she'll do squats all day.

She gets that she has body dysmorphia. She knows this intellectually. She knows further that societal body standards are garbage anyway. So logically, she can look at her lifestyle and label it STUPID. But, at a deeper level, her cells tell her she is RIGHT - her legs are definitely a problem. She feels it down to a cellular level. It's an even deeper truth than the pain.

Sometimes she wonders if she'd have less hip pain if she knew how to swivel her hips. She has the manliest walk. Her hips stay perfectly level. She developed this walk at age 14, not at all consciously, but she learned that the more her hips swivel, the more the thighs jiggle—a feeling akin to death. She was descending into deep anorexia, and her thought patterns were solidifying without intention.

Her disorder created all kinds of highly masculine mannerisms. She walks with her legs wide apart—so that she never feels her thighs touch, a feeling that triggers dire panic. She's completely unladylike. Spread eagle, like a dude making room for his junk. But if her legs are together, a constant buzzing of you fucking fatty drowns out whatever social or work interaction she's attempting.

There's also a fear of exuding any sexuality when you hate your body so much. If you find yourself disgusting, the last thing you want is for anyone to be looking at you with sexual interest. For years, whenever the clothes were coming off with a man, a chorus of, "Holy shit, I am about to LET THIS GUY DOWN!" played on repeat in her mind.

She knows better than that now. She's still self-conscious about her body when clothes come off, but she accepts that her partner is not seeing what she feels. He's seeing what he wants to see.

This is happening now. As she tucks him into bed, he pulls her close. The movements hurt, but she wants it. It'll stop hurting as it goes – natural pain relievers are released when aroused. Some evolutionary trick to encourage a body to keep going. Procreate, damn you! the cells insist.

Afterwards the pain is worse.

He snores again. She takes the pills.

There isn't enough left here to kill me, is there.

Not that she is suicidal. Content to just entertain suicidal thoughts. She loves the game she plays when crossing the bridge over the interstate on foot. Tracking one car on the busy freeway below her until it collides with her body – were her body on the same level as the car. It's a phenomenal feeling. Watching the car glide towards her and then – boom –imaginary impact, ending it all. Erasing it all. What peace. What bliss. No more nerve endings screaming like a goddamn coven of banshees.

She watches the bedroom get brighter with the sunrise, signaling the reality of a day to get through. In the nighttime, sometimes one can pretend the day won't come. That one might die before it arrives. But that's not happening today. Gloria said not this year.

When he stirs in a few hours, she'll roll over to appear like she's been sleeping. Must communicate a sense of normalcy.

But for now, she remains corpse-like. Flat on her back, listening with her nerving endings, as her body screams at her.

About the Author: Kate Huffman is a Los Angeles-based writer and actor whose most recent work is her award-winning solo show, I'M TOO FAT FOR THIS SHOW, which she is currently touring nationally and internationally. Her work has earned her an Encore Producers' Award, an LA Weekly Theatre Award, a Los Angeles Drama Critics Circle nomination, a Soaring Solo nomination, and Playhouse West Film Festival Award for Best Screenplay Short Film. She takes a lot of prescription pills, but her heart's in the right place. For more: KateHuffman.com.

Website: KateHuffman.com
Facebook: https://www.facebook.com/kate.huffman.92
https://www.facebook.com/ImTooFatforThisShow/
Instagram:https://www.instagram.com/imtoofatforthisshow/
Twitter: https://twitter.com/kate_huffman

"The Zen of Anima"

by C. Angelo Caci

There are those "things" of life that lie just beyond our reach. I've come to believe they must. Otherwise, if everything we pined after were within our grasp, there would be nothing to aspire to; reaching would be nothing more than a routine, a perfunctory act devoid of passion. Sometimes it's the reaching without the grasping that keeps us going. This is what I've come to believe. And it was on Palm Street, Venice, California that one such instance occurred. By the way, this was when I lived in Venice some years back, and wherein I must say, to some extent, mine heart still dwells — sometimes. It was with She. Don't even know her name — never did. Just she. She, who lived not far away from me either, as a matter of fact. She, of whom I'd lusted over all the while I'd lived there — privately, I mean. Unbeknownst to me, she was waitressing at Paolo's Italian Cuisine on Palm Street, which was much to my surprise, and delight, when I'd entered. I was only at Paolo's restaurant the one time. I never returned. After all, I'm not a total glutton for punishment. I'm not referencing the cuisine either. Patience, dear reader, as you'll soon see what I mean. I can remember to this day even, and with such astute clarity, the aura of red lust on green envy capriccio.

The décor at Paolo's is predictable, nothing fancy. In fact, the décor, as I remember, was little more than let's pretend we're in Italia. Not very convincing either, all told. I can safely say this even though I'd never been to Italia, and in all likelihood never will —doesn't matter. The placemats there are all silkscreened with each one featuring a different photograph of Venezia, Italia. I was somewhat bemused at the time, you might say, and not without more than just an element of fantasia simply because I'd never noticed the similarities of the canals of Venice to the canals of Venice (Venezia). I was also quite stoned as well . . . and famished. I thought while engrossed in the picture of the Canale Grande that despite Huxley's expanding universe this might very well be observed to be a rather shrinking one instead. I say this because I'd thought that I'd recognized a house that a friend lived in on Grand Canal on the placemat. Quite impossible. Anyway, while I'm perusing the canals in a gondola upon the placemat I'm ever so gently drawn from this muse by this very attractive waitress — She, as I've alluded to, whom I'd lusted over for so very, very long. Sumptuously outfitted in a black miniskirt, she'd inquired as to what I'd like, or if I'd like something or other, and indeed did I wont. However, what inevitably must have been interpreted by her as an affirmation that I did indeed want — ahh, if she only knew — she'd whirled about with the ease of an accomplished dancer, and I was heretofore very beneficently granted a twinkle, just a twinkle mind you, of such salacious creamy innerthigh, enduringly enough, despite that fact that this twinkle didn't even last long enough to finish its twink!

I'd resolved with the speed of a quantum leap to the target of my appetite, and did so without even a glance at the menu beforehand. I intuitively knew I'd order something, anything, ala Alfredo. Go figure? After her disappearance in a cloud of steam, having passed through a pair of double-swinging doors into the realm of the kitchen — which de facto appeared to me as Dante's infernal where all pleasures of the flesh simmer and bubble releasing the musks of tantalizing, gluttonous, proclivities — she'd reappeared with some cool, lemony, expunge served in a tall glass and perspiring with cascades of droplets all of which seemed to contain, and telegraph to me, subliminal messages of caprice.

"Thank you." I must have gasped this, as she'd cocked her head just so, as if she'd noticed my zipper was down, exposing the lewd undertones narrating my pant. Her reaction caused a wave of angel hair *al dente* to cascade down her delicate and slender mostaccioli neck, and it's no doubt because of this vision that caused me to have ordered angel hair pasta, but of course. Also, of course, Alfredo sauce, as well as a side of creamed spinach. Despite the fact that I didn't remember even ordering, I nonetheless must assume I did simply because this is what she brought me. Surprise surprise!

Anyway, the ensalada placed in front of me to the left of my creamed Bathsheba contained a generous portion of pine nuts, two very supple olives, and one nubile, yet old enough to eat, cherry tomato that I'd uncovered, and indeed undressed, beneath a bikini-sized leaf of lettuce. I remember this distinctly. And, I must have done more than just tip-toe through this garden salad, and done so to the apparent amusement of my winged, angel-haired, provocateur, as I'd not even noticing the warm, sweet-glaze of the young, spring-nectar of the pride of Venice upon my puss afterward. She did. I think so anyway. I thought I'd caught what surely resembled a smirk upon her face as I'm sure the marinara-tint of embarrassment upon mine didn't go unnoticed either. Could she have known? Anyway, after I'd shamelessly indulged, I compensated by telling myself that the price of all this splendor in the green was only a couple bucks more than a big and sloppy quickie from the wide-spread, cholesteroled, thighs of McGreasyland. I was, after all, on a budget those years.

I vowed to return. Perhaps next time I'll order something Calabrese, or perhaps even Siciliano, and free myself of social inhibitions, plunge into my carnal nature as I shamelessly gorge on the fresh kill of the illusive and fleeting meatballs, or perhaps the wild sausages of wildebeest. Shed of shyness, I'll toast to the finest local-grown … the scent of a sprig of spring basil, the voluptuous, leafy limbs of oregano intertwined in a passionate and nude embrace with a virgin bathed in olive oil … Oh, but to wallow in the primordial ooze of creamed spinach, even if only bathed in just a hint of her mint.

As I'd stated, I'd never returned. Simply because. But I've never really left either.

©2017 C. Angelo Caci

About the Author: A bio, or portrait of the artist, would best be conveyed in a literary still life: laptop with reading lamp clamped to the lid, Merlot in a cut-glass goblet, a pack of Garcia Vegas, or Grenadiers, and a pair of reading glasses set on its lenses with one obtrusive stem slightly twisted sticking straight up and readied.

"Omael"

by Joyce Stein

Judith loved the beach: the sun, sound, and sand, but not so much the water. She had issues with its size, strength and depth. Other than that, the beach was her place of solace. It wiped away the horrible jobs, the errant boyfriends and her poor life choices. She had made it a ritual. Going every day to the same beach, the same spot, for years. Occasionally, she'd wet her toes.

On this particular day, she noticed a man waving at her in the water, a distance from shore. She squinted. She hoped he didn't need help because she was not the one. He waved again and smiled. Drowning men don't generally smile. She waved, turned her back to him and laid down on her stomach.

The following day he appeared again, only a little closer to shore. He waved. Odd; she had never seen him before. Judith appreciated his look: honey brown, sun-kissed with golden dreads, and a swim suit slung so low that only the water was keeping his privates private. But it was definitely showing off his wash-board abs. She resisted the urge to wave back, but she could not divert her eyes. There was something basic, primal, and hedonistic about him. She felt a spike in her body temperature and it had nothing to do with the sun. When Judith finally waved back, he beckoned her to him. She shook her head no. Maybe it wasn't that deep, maybe he was really tall, or maybe he was a serial killer who liked to drown his victims. Judith stood up, shouted no and gave a crossed slash of her arms (was that a nautical sign?). Ok, she also stood up just in case he was not a serial killer. Maybe her assets would bring him to shore.

The next day, he was nowhere to be found. Serial killer, most definitely, a serial killer, but Judith could not keep her eyes off the horizon. She skipped the beach the following day. It was against protocol and sacrilegious. What if he never showed up again?

Returning to her spot the day after, Judith kept her back to the waves. The sun was what she really needed. She heard a splash, but didn't turn. Multiple sounds: voices, sea gulls, and waves, lulled her into a deep sleep. She was awakened by a trough of wet trash thrown onto her backside. Judith jumped up. The dread man glistened in the water, close to shore. She ran forward.

"Did you do that?" she shouted. He merely shrugged, smiled and beckoned to her again. "I told you, I'm not coming out there."

He shrugged again and pushed up on his arms, exposing his chest. Judith eyed him. He smiled. She was at water's edge and could see his eyes. What color was that? Green? Hazel? Blue? She edged closer to the water. He kept smiling, holding out both hands and coaxing her to him.

She tried again, "I'm afraid of deep water." He put his hand over his heart and then extended it to her. Judith went out to him.

Just as she reached him, she noticed something odd. The bottom half of him was not visible in the waterline. That was impossible. She was only waist deep. She hesitated. He smiled. Then, she saw a huge fish tail smack the water just behind him. She turned, screaming, but he grabbed her by the waist and pulled her under.

Judith lost count of how many times he surfaced. She'd scream and he'd dive. Eventually, she stopped screaming, but by that time they were miles out to sea. In an act of pure defiance, she batted his hands away. She could tread water, kind of. He respected her wishes, let go and sunk to eye level. She suspected he was studying her, laughing at her. Judith treaded, struggled and then sank. When he eventually retrieved her, she had only one question, "Why?"

He pulled her to him and kissed her gently on every surface above water. Judith had long since lost any hint of a swim suit. She felt all his textures, muscles and heat against her bare skin. He didn't feel scaly as much as he did leathery. She wasn't sure what to do with her hands. She looked directly in his eyes. Mistake. They were beautiful, kind, loving and gentle. He smiled again, pushed her hair back and then gently held it kissing her chest. Judith had a sudden thought, drowning might not be such a bad way to go.

That night, Judith attempted conversation multiple times. Her man-fish only shrugged and smiled. He swam her out to places she would never have ventured, but eventually brought her clinging body back to shore. Standing in the waves, she pointed to herself and said,

"Judith." He took her hand and fingered spelled letters into the palm of her hand,

"O M A E L."

Judith looked up into his eyes, "Your name is Omael? He nodded, smiled and kissed her. That was a good name, but with a kiss like that it hardly mattered.

Just before releasing her, Omael gave Judith another signal. A hand to the sky, with a falling angle. "Tomorrow night?" Judith guessed. He nodded. She nodded, then he was gone.

Judith waited on the beach the following day, from twilight into darkness. She studied the constellations until the full moon brightened the sky. No Omael. She sighed. What could she have done with a man-fish, anyway? She settled back and absorbed the silence.

Packing up, Judith thought she heard a splash. She stopped and turned. There was Omael, walking slowly towards her wearing a very scant cover of seaweed, water dripping from his dreads. She was so stunned she could neither move nor make a sound. A man-fish was one thing, a real man on land was another.

As Omael reached her, he gently took her into his arms and kissed her softly. "Judith," he whispered in a low husky voice. Judith felt her knees go weak. He pressed her to him. "It's ok," he reassured her, "I am allowed to become human if I desire on the first night of the full moon. I desired it. Now make me yours."

Judith was having a hard time gathering her wits. Omael's hands were caressing every inch of her body and his lips were claiming every section of her neck and shoulder line. Why resist? She wrapped her arms around him. Suddenly, he broke free. "Let's go," he sighed. He took her hand and she led him to her place. Omael pushed all the curtains and shades aside, flooding her apartment in moonlight. And there, in all its beauty and brightness, he took her.

The following morning, Omael was gone. There was a fine grit of sand and the scent of salt on her sheets. She exhaled loudly and plodded to the bathroom. There in the tub was a pile of seaweed with a large fractal seashell on top. She ran her hand slowly over the seaweed, held the shell to her ear and smiled.

©2017 Joyce Stein

About the Author: In my mind, I'm an artist and a writer. In my reality, I'm a registered nurse, avid gardener, grandmother, wife and mother. The lines get blurred sometimes, but that's part of the fun. I completed my first novel this summer and am currently pitching it to agents. My technology skills are poor, but I'm happy to say that I've almost given up paper and pencils and am trying to write directly on my computer. I love the creative process, whether sorting through fabrics, paint and trim, building and re-arranging garden beds or researching and collecting words, names and ideas. I'm a persistent dreamer, so I'm still working on making all my dreams come true.

"To Know Again Why it is You Have Come"

by Keren Heenan

You know you have to get up tomorrow and do it all over again and you don't think you can with your feet feeling like every bone is broken and you wonder if you might need a hip replacement too when you get back home but you get up off the bed and stand and moan and put one foot after the other and think of the wine the paella your friends waiting for you or perhaps they're not waiting at all but dragging their aching bodies around in their rooms thinking of tomorrow and how they'll have to walk another twenty or thirty kilometres again and thinking of the wine and paella so that when you get to the bar you'll all be there at the same time showered and changed yet bleary-eyed and cactus with seemingly broken-bone feet and muscles so tight they wrap like an iron girdle around your thighs and you'll all fall over each other trying to get to the wine first so you can just sit upright at the table and not want to lie prone on the floor or a bench seat with eyes closed and a sort of white haze in your head that keeps insinuating itself into your present in a sort of what the hell are you doing here and do you think you can possibly go on but then it will come as it always does the memory of the walk the hills all bald and green and sweeping and the drift of fog over the valleys below the thin ribbon of the trail on the next hill and the passing pilgrims with their Buen Camino! and it's just enough to keep you going with the hills so steep that they force you to look down at your feet at the ant just passing your boot the beetles the pebbles the flattened moss on the path dendritic like tree roots like twigs like the veins in your body and one lonely purple flower per- sisting in a pebbled dry brown landscape or the fat black slugs as thick as a man's thumb and at least ten centimetres long inching their way across the dusty surface and the roadside adorned with wild strawberries blackberry bushes tangled bracken fennel and rosehips olives grapevines chestnut trees and walnuts or almonds and you forget the sun beating down and the ache in your hips the sweat on your upper lip in rivulets between your breasts and in your eyes and your glasses sliding down your nose forget that you'd wanted to give up not thinking of the distance already covered or how each step takes you closer and even though you know there will be no falling to your knees when you arrive in Santiago de Compostela you know that the silence and struggle of the walk will all mean something in the end and that you will want to live this unrushed rhythm this life of walking perhaps forever and that the world you will return to with all its perceived urgency will not be like the slow nothingness and silence of your head in the clouds the path beneath your feet so you make your way down the three flights of stairs trying hard to look like the sort of person who would contemplate walking nearly eight hundred kilometres across the top of Spain over the Pyrenees for godsakes! well the foothills at least and then on and on and up and up then down that knee jerking descent into the village on that first day and now it's just down three flights of stairs and of course you can do this simple walk though you are sure your ankle is twice its size and your knee has that old odd ache that comes and goes and is now more coming than going and then you're there and they're sitting waiting after all and they turn as one and you all give the look that says what the hell have we got ourselves into and like an ancient crone you drag yourself over to the table and sit carefully arranging your thighs and hips into a comfortable position and lean your elbows on the table and sigh and you all sigh then laugh so loud heads turn and the bottles of wine arrive and it's like the elixir to combat all struggles has been delivered and you all raise glasses and drink and laugh and remember the reasons why you're all here and none of the ones that could let the gloom take you knowing that you are a team with these three and you remember the wind turbines cutting lazy arcs through the warm air the chiming bells on cows and goats and unicycle man on the path and the dogs and the woman pushing a pram and the young Italian boys with their jerseys open to the breast bone flashing past on their smooth fast bikes the road signs that always seem to indicate further distance than you'd thought possible given how far you'd already come and the great mound of sorrow at Cruz de Ferro they'd said take a stone of your sorrows and leave it there how it took you by surprise the ferocity of it the weight there beneath your feet in the pebbles the rocks the photos and plastic bracelets and cards and religious mementos the footsteps echoing back through the centuries full with the lives lost and how we are all that sorrow all human all one and then the girl in tears because she'd lost not one but five and you'd hugged her a stranger and didn't ask for details that's not what she wanted just to know that we are all one we are all in this together all struggling blistered and sunburnt and human and telling ourselves we can do this we can go on because Life is El Camino with all its hills and valleys and wild beauty and pain and you walk yourself into the glory of a sunset that stains crimson and apricot over the brow of the hill and you know again why it is you have come.

©2017 Keren Heenan

About the Author: Keren Heenan is a writer and Arts teacher living in Melbourne Australia. She is the winner of a number of Australian short story awards and placed 2nd in the Fish Prize 2015. She has been published in Australian journals and anthologies, including: Overland, Island, Wet Ink, Award Winning Australian Writing, in Aesthetica Creative Writing Annual (UK) 2014 and Fish Anthology 2015.

"Two Sisters"

by J. Peters

I cowered into the jumbled array of blankets and sheets; shivering, chattering, frozen.

"Hypothermia?"

"No, no, we won't let that happen. The roads are blocked. We need to deal with this."

She tightened the blankets around me, threw more logs on the fire and told the other girl to cook some food.

"That's Sue, my step-sister. I'm Jen. You were very brave out there. The blizzard would have killed us if it wasn't for you."

I croaked out my name in response. My limbs seared with pain. The noises around me drifted further away.

When I awoke, an aroma fed my senses. Jen was crouched over me holding a bottle and a bowl; warm water droplets that made me salivate, then soft chewy meat in a soupy mix.

Liquid trickled down my chin. She pressed her thumb around and under my lower lip, then popped it into her mouth. Sucking and licking noises swam through my thoughts reminding me of something luscious, but the memory stayed out of reach.

Weariness dragged me lower into the bed. Each time I opened my eyes she was looking at me. I ate ravenously; coals into a steam engine fuelling the burning sensations. Sated, I dozed off.

I heard soft voices come and go; felt hard ice inside me that refused to thaw. I had no sense of time.

"We need … something else."

Glorious heat seeped into my bones; they were each side of me, pressed close, their breath on my cheeks and legs over mine. Clasped hands lay on my belly and fingers trailed lightly through my hair. Energy radiated through me.

I tried to speak, but Jen placed a long, sleek finger on my lips while whispering escaped hers. "You still need rest. You look feverish."

I nodded. Sue lay on my chest, and I instinctively placed my hand over her. Jen sidled in closer, her cheek against mine. Yielding softness pulled me into a deeper sleep.

Movement all around me, then on me; some of the heaviness peeled away. They were speaking in hushed, worried tones.

More voices, but they were lighter this time. Something felt different; smooth, delectable, skin on skin. They were both naked, rubbing me all over, generating more sublime heat. My mind was still hazy, but I reacted to their proximity. When I opened my eyes, they were leaning over me, smiling.

Sue cradled my face and pressed her hand over my midriff. "You look a lot better now, and you feel a lot better too." She peppered me with little kisses.

Shadows danced on the walls; crackling logs sent them scurrying lower. My cheeks were burning from more than silken kisses.

We were beneath a sheet so I could see no more of them. Jen's legs lay against mine, one on top and one to the side, tantalisingly open. She fed me again - nourishing, rejuvenating, revitalising me. With each spoonful she slid into my mouth, her breasts brushed my chest, and her labia grazed against my hip. I wanted her to sit on my face.

I ate slowly and enjoyed watching her tongue curling around her lips as if she was eating with me.

Sue dabbed her fingers in more water and trailed it over me. When she lingered, I exhaled the sensation in the pit of my stomach and stifled a moan through more mouthfuls of pleasure.

"Are you warm enough?"

I could only nod.

When Jen finished feeding me, she slid out from under the sheet. I caught her scent as I inhaled; light and musky. Her thighs glistened.

I watched her as she walked away; swinging hips and a curvy ass. My mouth went dry as she returned. I gulped down the last morsel and stifled an urge to jump her.

"You're too warm now, aren't you?"

Sue had my attention again. "Shall I take the sheet off?"

Without waiting for an answer, she flung it back.

Both were standing, legs apart, pulling my gaze into their smoothness. Pert breasts with erect nipples partially covered by long hair; hips that made my eyes curl. Hard bellies and long legs I wanted to trace. Pussies I wanted to fuck.

"A massage will help you feel better."

When they giggled, I buried my head in the pillow to hold the vibrations there; I shivered through the resonance.

Warm oil dripped over my weary limbs; their hands rubbed it into me, and I felt more ripples up my spine. They parted my legs and brushed over the insides of my thighs.

Warmth flooded my midriff when fingernails slithered across my belly; I closed my eyes when they both kissed there. Sloppy sounds, wetness, as Jen inched towards my neck and Sue meandered lower.

Thoughts of coldness were banished. When Jen reached my mouth, I strangled a cry in my throat. She climbed on top, her breasts heavy on me, tongue thrust around mine. Spasms of pleasure as Sue's hands stroked me; then she reached between Jen's legs and played with her too. When they both moaned my name, my desire became violent. I smothered a need to dominate them.

Then a feather brushed over us and between our legs. Something leather-like tickled me, and I squirmed underneath her. More licking and biting, until I felt Jen oozing onto me; her moisture sliding along Sue's tongue, dripping down the insides of my thighs.

Sweat trickled down Jen's back. Two different kinds of breathless fed my quivers; one radiated hot and rough in my mouth, the other cool breeze between my legs. Faster they sucked and teased; Jen rocking above me, moaning my name, then Sue's.

I grabbed Sue's hand and our fingers interlaced as we shot inside Jen's heat, spilling more luxurious moisture over my belly and legs. I slid further under her that I could see Sue biting into us. When I grabbed Jen's breasts, I twisted and sucked hard until she came. Her spasms flowed through me like waves as I came too – my moisture sucked into the wet, stickiness of Sue's mouth.

Jen whispered in my ear as our orgasms ripped through us. "I want you again, Liv!"

"Me too," I whispered back. My fingernails dug into her as I arched further into Sue. When the ripples stopped, we were drenched in sweat.

I looked at them. Moisture, still on Sue's lips, flamed my command.

"Lie on top of each other."

The thought of licking both clits made me weak. I felt the heat rise inside me again as I slid my tongue into Sue, then Jen, fingering both of them too. When I felt them kissing up against my ass, I almost fainted.

As both girls entered me, I squirted into them; light-headed and fiery to the core.

©2017 J. Peters

About the Author: J.Peters, an emerging writer living in Ireland, loves reading and writing. You can follow J.Peters on facebook.

"The Drummonds"

by Joyce Stein

Marking the winter solstice, Dr. Bertha Ann Johnson officially became Mrs. Angus Muir Drummond on December 21, 2017. The ceremony and reception were held at Castello di Amorosa, in California's Napa Valley. Angus wore a traditional kilt as befitting his Scottish clan, while Bertha donned a golden lace Nigerian wedding dress with an elaborate head wrap. They were stunning.

The couple grew up on the same block and met in grade school. Frankly, they could not stand each other. It wasn't until Bertha accidently backed over Angus while attempting to sneak out with her family's car that they really got to know each other. As punishment for borrowing the vehicle without permission, driving without a license and being out past curfew, Bertha was assigned to care for Angus until he was out of his full leg cast. Two weeks into the recovery, Angus had made Bertha cry multiple times, and he was not sorry one little bit. Thanks to her, his senior year on the football team was over. Once he got over his anger and she got over her humiliation, things really started to happen. By week four they had stopped calling each other names and began doing homework together. Both found neither was as dunce as each had presumed. Eight weeks in, Angus convinced Bertha he needed a bed bath. The loofah scrubbing she gave him, left him bright red with multiple abrasions, but he enjoyed every minute of it. His parents, Reverend Peter and Priscilla Drummond, formerly from Harrisburg, Pennsylvania, however, were not amused. They did not appreciate these new injuries nor how they were incurred. Bertha's final four weeks of Angus' care was terminated. Her parents, Professors Ralph and Martha Johnson of Los Angeles, agreed with the Drummonds and Bertha spent that summer down south with her grandmother.

The experience taught Bertha that she enjoyed caring for people. She went to UC Berkeley, was accepted to their medical school, and became a family practice MD. Angus was able to return to his beloved football, walked-on to USC, received a full scholarship the following year, and was the number ten draft pick to quarterback for the Raiders, with whom he continues to play.

Bertha and Angus reconnected on a dare from a mutual friend that implied he would not go out with someone so hued, while she would not go out with someone so fair. It was a blind date. They were shocked to find out it was each other. In their combined history together, they had never really noticed their shades. He admitted that he thought she was a snotty bitch, while her memory of him was as a pompous jock. It was an awkward beginning, but a few drinks in and of course, after the retelling of the loofah scrub, things settled in. Bertha challenged his memory of the event, admitting to him being shirtless but denying further knowledge of the extent of his ginger-ism. She had quirked an eyebrow at him and he had choked on a French fry. It was then that he knew she was the girl for him. Several hours later, after an impromptu dinner and a night cap, they walked the beach until sunrise. They've been together ever since. What they've found in each other is a sense of adventure, comfortable companionship, deep love and a strong friendship.

In honoring their love, uniqueness and diversity all guests were requested to attend in cultural costumes, with the hope that everyone would embrace their historical background, research and learn some new ancestry, or just experience a different dimension. Those not in requested attire were not permitted on the property

The bride was walked down the aisle escorted by her mother and father. The groom's father stood as his best man. The ceremony was officiated by a Scottish priest, also dressed in a kilt. The bride would later joke that she did not understand a word he said. She had only said 'I do' when Angus slipped the twenty carat ring on her finger and everyone looked at her. There was a small disruption when someone attempted to say why they should not be joined. They were taken out by the offensive line guests. Bertha never got to see who was causing the fuss. The couple shared a long lingering kiss, then jumped the broom together.

Photos were taken throughout the castle and in the accompanying vineyards and gardens. There was very little traditional about the shoot. The bride and groom photo featured Angus seated on a black stead with Bertha on his lap. The defensive line in kilts made quite the impression, while the bride's maids lounging on harem pillows raised a few eyebrows. The parents and family photo were quite quaint, but the bridal party picture turned into a series of unposed frames that included men in women's laps, women on men's backs and the entire party on horses, carts and wagons.

Since the winter solstice is the longest night of the year, not a second of it was wasted. The festivities began with ribald questions reference the men of honor being in kilts and what is worn under them. A few women received some quick flashes and from their re-actions and coloring, the rumor must be true. The bride's maids, dressed in a variation of African and Middle Eastern wear, broke out into a wild combo African belly dance, so as not to be outdone. The men joined the women and soon the room was ablaze with swirling colors. People were still trying to locate their seats for the reception.

There was a live band, throw-back music, circle dancing, and a conga line. It is rumored that food and flowers were flown in from every part of the globe and that the champagne flowed non-stop. Since all the guests had accommodations on the grounds, there was little need for limitation nor discretion.

The bride and groom snuck out before sunrise to begin their honeymoon. They are scheduled for a four-week, unscripted world tour of romantic cities, tropical islands and historical wonder site destinations.

©2017 Joyce Stein

About the Author: In my mind, I'm an artist and a writer. In my reality, I'm a registered nurse, avid gardener, grandmother, wife and mother. The lines get blurred sometimes, but that's part of the fun. I completed my first novel this summer and am currently pitching it to agents. My technology skills are poor, but I'm happy to say that I've almost given up paper and pencils and am trying to write directly on my computer. I love the creative process, whether sorting through fabrics, paint and trim, building and re-arranging garden beds or researching and collecting words, names and ideas. I'm a persistent dreamer, so I'm still working on making all my dreams come true.

About Two Sisters
Writing and Publishing:

We are sisters — Elizabeth Ann Atkins and Catherine Marie Atkins Greenspan. We write and publish our own books, we blog, we ghost-write memoirs for accomplished people, we teach a writing method called PowerJournal, and we celebrate other writers through our monthly short story contests. We feature award-winning stories on our website, and you're holding the first anthology of our fabulous writers from 2016 and 2017.

Please see more stories at www.twosisterswriting.com.

Books Published By
Two Sisters Writing and Publishing

"CLEAR!" Living the Life You Didn't Dream Of

~Herman Williams, MD

My Name is Steve Delano Bullock:
How I Changed My World
and the World Around Me
through Leadership,
Caring, and Perseverance

~Steve D. Bullock

Let the Future Begin

~ Dennis W. Archer

The Triumph of Rosemary: A Memoir

~ Judge Marylin E. Atkins

Dark Secret (re-release)

~ Elizabeth Ann Atkins

The Veronica Series

Veronica, I Heard Your Mom's Black

Veronica Talks to Boys

Race Home, Veronica

~ Catherine M. Greenspan

Forthcoming Books

God's Answer is Know

~ Elizabeth Ann Atkins

The Veronica Series

Grace Under Pressure

Sally's Indoor Fiesta

Hey, Jude, Is that White Lady Your Mom?

~ Catherine M. Greenspan

We're Standing By

~ Al Allen

Remembering and Forgetting:
a spiritual journey

~ Lin Day

The Making Point

~ US Army Master Sgt. Cedric King

A.M. Total Being Fitness Journal

~ Anthony Moses

Confessions of a Plastic Surgeon:
Shocking Secrets about Enhancing
Butts, Boobs, and Beauty

~ Thomas T. Jeneby, MD

First Annual Anthology

The Enemy Within

~ Michael Wood, MD

~ Elizabeth Ann Atkins

Twilight (re-release)

~ Billy Dee Williams

~ Elizabeth Ann Atkins

www.ingramcontent.com/pod-product-compliance
Lightning Source LLC
Chambersburg PA
CBHW032014180726
48283CB00008B/2671